PRETTY IN PINK

Stevie crossed her stirrups over Belle's saddle and followed Max's instructions. She was used to this exercise, and she was good at it. She also knew it was extremely useful and effective. She only wished they had more time to work with it.

Instead, the class had been spent paying a lot of attention to Miss Pink Jodhpurs and her "li'l ole horse." Sure, she knew what she was doing, but what was the point? Nobody rode sidesaddle anymore. Why would anyone want to?

Stevie recognized the darkness of her own mood, but there seemed little she could do to lighten it up. The fact that the rest of the class was oohing and aahing at Tiffani's ability to ride sidesaddle without a stirrup didn't help at all.

The end of class couldn't come soon enough.

THE SADDLE CLUB

SIDESADDLE

BONNIE BRYANT

A SKYLARK BOOK
NEW YORK · TORONTO · LONDON · SYDNEY · AUCKLAND

Special thanks to Sir "B" Farms
and Laura and Vinny Marino

RL 5, 009–012

SIDESADDLE
A Bantam Skylark Book / July 1999

ISBN 0-553-48673-X

Published simultaneously in the United States and Canada

Bantam Books are published by Bantam Books, a division of Random
House, Inc. Its trademark, consisting of the words "Bantam Books" and the
portrayal of a rooster, is Registered in U.S. Patent and Trademark Office
and in other countries. Marca Registrada. Bantam Books, 1540 Broadway,
New York, New York 10036.

PRINTED IN THE UNITED STATES OF AMERICA
OPM   0 9 8 7 6 5 4 3 2 1

In memory of Neil

"DID YOU BRING ANY carrots?" Lisa Atwood asked Stevie Lake, one of her two best friends, as they walked together toward Pine Hollow Stables. It was a summery Saturday morning in the spring, and that meant they were on their way to a meeting of Horse Wise, their Pony Club. Any trip to the stable meant a visit with horses, and horses loved carrots.

"Oh, I'm sure I did," Stevie said, digging into the pocket of her riding jeans. Her fingers found the carrots there, all right, but the fact that they were rubbery gave her the sinking feeling that they'd been there since the last riding class—on Wednesday.

"Well, sort of," she said, adjusting her previous answer. She drew two limp orange sticks out of her pocket. "I think I'll spare the horses that joy." She tossed the carrots into the tall grass at the edge of the street that led to Pine Hollow.

"I guess it's a good thing I remembered some fresh ones," Lisa teased, pulling a bag of carrots out of her backpack. "Be nice to me and I'll let you give some of these to Belle."

"I'm always nice to you," Stevie said. "In fact, I'm always nice to everybody." Her hazel eyes sparkled mischievously in the morning sunlight.

Lisa laughed. If there was one thing about Stevie, it was that she was *not* always nice to everyone. She was almost always nice to people she liked, but if someone irked her, she was more than capable of playing practical jokes that were anything but nice.

However, Stevie *was* usually nice to her two best friends. She and Lisa, along with Carole Hanson, were nearly inseparable. As soon as the three girls had discovered their common bond, they'd formed a group they called The Saddle Club. It had only two rules. The first was the easy part: Members had to be horse-crazy. The second rule was that they had to be willing to help one another out. Quite often that meant that Carole and Lisa found themselves supporting one of the wild schemes that Stevie was inclined to invent. Sometimes it meant helping her get out of the hot water those wild schemes often got her into.

Stevie was simply irrepressible. Once she set her mind to something, there was little that could stop her, and her friends had long since discovered that their weakest weapon against her imagination was common sense.

Common sense was something Lisa was loaded with. Compared to Stevie, she was the national repository of common sense. She used a logical approach to problem solving, rather than Stevie's emotional one. She was clearheaded in almost any situation. These qualities tended to balance Stevie's in their friendship. They also gave Lisa the tools she needed to be a straight-A student. Everything about Lisa was calm and logical. Her light brown hair was always neatly combed, while Stevie's hair seemed to evade every attempt she made to capture it. Lisa's clothes were always clean and neatly pressed, while Stevie's apparel was more frequently retrieved from her closet's quasi–laundry pile. Lisa's clothes were fashionable and carefully coordinated—she'd be likely to wear a navy blue sweater and a white blouse with a blue-and-white-checked skirt. Stevie's outfits tended to be coordinated with whatever was on the top of that laundry pile—she'd wear her patched blue jeans with her older brother's cast-off T-shirt and a pair of socks stealthily borrowed from her twin brother. Stevie was definitely not fashionable. The best her mother could usually come up with to say about her wardrobe was "interesting."

Stevie and Lisa were as different from one another as they were from Carole. Decidedly the horse-craziest of the three girls, Carole was totally organized when it came to horses and more than a little flaky when it came to everything else. Carole always knew exactly where her riding clothes were, but she might not be so certain about her social studies homework. She could answer complicated questions at Horse Wise about the seasonal changes in equine diet, but she might forget that she'd promised her father she'd make brownies for dessert.

A horn honked behind Lisa and Stevie just as they arrived at the stable driveway. They turned to see Colonel Hanson's station wagon delivering Carole to Pine Hollow. Colonel Hanson stopped his car and let Carole out, giving her a quick kiss, so that she could join her friends for the last part of the walk to the Pony Club meeting.

The girls began chatting easily on their favorite topic: horses.

"Max said there was going to be something special today," Lisa said.

"What can be so special at an unmounted meeting?" Stevie asked. She loved learning all there was to learn about horses, but she was always happier when she was learning it in a saddle.

"Unmounted meetings aren't so bad," Carole said, barely acknowledging that her father was driving off. "I mean, remember how interesting all that stuff was about pesticides last time?"

Only Carole would find pesticides interesting, Stevie thought. Oh, sure they were important, necessary, even essential. But interesting? Not in her opinion.

"I don't think he meant more pesticides," Lisa said. "It's something else. And it has to do with the class, too."

The Horse Wise meeting on Saturday morning was usually followed by a picnic lunch and then a riding class. That meant that almost all of Saturday was devoted to horses. To Lisa, Stevie, and Carole, that meant that almost all of Saturday was pretty special, particularly when they could follow it up with a visit to their favorite ice cream shop and a sleepover at one of their houses.

"Well, then, we'd better hurry," Carole said, picking up her pace.

"Morning, girls."

"Good morning, Mrs. Reg," they said, greeting the stable manager, who also happened to be the mother of their riding instructor and Pony Club director, Max Regnery.

Mrs. Reg had a look in her eye that said there were chores to be done. It was, actually, a look she almost always had in her eye, because at Pine Hollow, as at any stable, there were always chores to be done, everything from feeding, watering, and grooming horses to mucking out stalls and cleaning tack. Horses were a lot of work, and the riders at Pine Hollow were never allowed to forget that. They learned that looking after their horses and ponies was every bit as important as riding them. Everyone was expected to pitch in. It was a way to learn. It was also a way to keep costs down so that the riders' families could have some relief from the expenses of riding and maintaining horses.

"We don't want to be late for the meeting," Lisa said, hoping that might get them out of a dirty mucking job.

"This'll just take a minute," said Mrs. Reg.

Lisa and Carole were invited to bring a bale of hay down from the loft. "And Stevie, can you help the new rider rinse out the trough in the ring?"

"Sure," Stevie said. She didn't mind. Everybody helped. Well, almost everybody. Pine Hollow had one rider who thought she was too good to help, that she didn't need to help, that other people had been born to perform her chores: Veronica diAngelo. If Mrs. Reg asked Veronica to do something, she would always agree sweetly and then turn around and give the task to someone else. Her favorite victim was Red O'Malley, the head stable hand.

As far as Stevie was concerned, it was too nice a morning to let anything get her down—including thoughts of Veronica. She'd rinse the trough in ten minutes, and that would leave her ample time to get to Max's office for the start of the meeting.

As these thoughts flashed through Stevie's mind, the words Mrs. Reg had actually said began to register: "the new rider." Making her way through the barn to the ring, greeting the horses she passed on her way, Stevie began to wonder.

Pine Hollow was in Willow Creek, Virginia, about twenty miles outside Washington, D.C. Because of the high turnover in government jobs in Washington, people were always moving into and out of Willow Creek, so there were often new faces at Pine Hollow. Stevie liked meeting new people. She had a natural rapport with all kinds of people. So she wondered about the new rider.

She didn't have to wonder long. The new rider was pointing a hose at the trough and doing her best to loosen the accumulated grunge.

"Mrs. Reg doesn't usually give such ucky jobs to new riders," Stevie said, approaching the girl. "Here, let me give you a hand."

The girl turned off the water and stood up to meet Stevie's gaze. "Oh, she didn't give me the job. I just saw that it was dirty and offered," she said.

"Good move," said Stevie. "I guarantee you've won your way into Mrs. Reg's heart. Hello, my name is Stevie Lake." She took the other girl's offered hand and shook it, though it felt odd to shake the hand of someone her own age.

"Tiffani Thomas," the girl said. "Do you think that brush over by the barn will help?"

Stevie looked. It was exactly what they needed. She went to fetch the long-handled brush. As she walked back, she couldn't believe that she hadn't noticed at first what Tiffani was wearing. They were riding clothes, all right, but not like any Stevie had ever seen, except for the highly polished black leather boots. Tiffani was wearing jodhpurs. Pink jodhpurs. Spotless pale pink jodhpurs. Stevie glanced down at her own dirty paddock boots and her riding jeans, already splashed with mud and water from the hose. And nothing that happened in the next ten minutes made Stevie one iota cleaner or Tiffani one single spot dirtier. It was amazing.

"I'm only here for a short time?" Tiffani said as they chatted about riding and Pine Hollow. "I really live in Tennessee, but my father had to go on a long trip and my mother wanted to go with him, so I'm staying with my aunt Jessie here in Willow Creek for this semester? I'm at Willow Creek Junior High?"

She wasn't really asking questions. It was just the way she spoke. Her lilting accent made every sentence sound like a question.

"Oh, I go to Fenton Hall," Stevie said. "I guess that's why we haven't met before."

"Right, well, and we haven't met here at Pine Hollow yet because my horse just got here. You wouldn't think it would be so complicated to ship a horse a couple of hundred miles, but I guess it is? I'd said to Mama and Daddy that there was no way I wasn't going to have Diamond with me. He just arrived on Thursday?"

"How great," Stevie said. "Well, I know you're going to love it here. Pine Hollow is great, and my two best friends go to Willow Creek—um, you'll meet them in just a minute."

Stevie made a final spray at the trough and then laid the running hose at its bottom to fill it up.

"Come on, let's get to the meeting. The first thing you're going to learn about Max is that he just hates it when people are late to his meetings and his classes."

Tiffani put the brush back where it had been, then told Stevie how glad she was to have someone there to show her the way. "It's just such a big old barn. I'm sure I'd get lost?"

"Oh, I don't think so, Tiffani," Stevie said. "All you have to do is follow your ears to where absolutely everybody is talking about horses!"

"Oh, Stevie, you're so funny!" Tiffani's laughter was light and musical. Stevie had never heard anything like it. She hadn't actually thought her joke was funny enough to merit musical laughter, but she realized that Tiffani was probably nervous. After all, she was in a strange place, among unfamiliar people, and her aunt had made her wear those awful jodhpurs today. That alone would have given Stevie hives at least, and there was no telling what it might have done to her laughter.

"Well, it's this way," she said, showing Tiffani how to get to Max's office. Max was waiting at the door.

"Oh, good, Stevie, you and Tiffani have already met. Then perhaps you could introduce her around to everyone."

Stevie didn't mind doing that. She introduced Tiffani first to Carole and Lisa and then to some of the others who were already there, including Veronica, Meg, April, Joe, May, Jasmine, and Corey. It turned out that Tiffani already knew April because they were in some classes together, so Stevie felt she could leave the two of them to talk while she returned to her own best friends.

"Pink?" Lisa whispered when Stevie sat down. Lisa was always perfectly dressed herself, but she almost never criticized what anybody else wore.

"Look, she's staying with her aunt here. She must have left her own jodhpurs at home in Tennessee, and this was all they could get at the last minute when her horse arrived," Stevie said. It was the only logical explanation.

Carole looked confused. "What are you two talking about?" she asked.

"Her clothes," Stevie whispered.

"She's got some on, doesn't she?" Carole asked.

10

Her friends grinned and rolled their eyes. Trust Carole not to notice something as noticeable as pink jodhpurs.

"Well, did you hear about her horse?" Carole asked.

"What about her horse?"

"Max told me she's got a Tennessee walking horse," Carole said. "They're a great breed, you know. They're related to Saddlebreds and have a number of things in common. They were specially bred to be pleasure riders, which is true of Saddlebreds, too. Their gaits are unique, though, and smooth as glass. The idea was that their owners should be able to spend a whole day in the saddle while riding around their plantations. There's something called the running walk. The hind feet overstep the front ones by more than a foot! Maybe she'd let me try him out sometime. I've ridden walkers before, but I don't think we've had one boarding here since—well, I guess there was one . . ."

Lisa and Stevie exchanged glances. It was totally typical of Carole to ignore pink riding pants in favor of talking about an unusual breed of horse. In fact, if there had been a horse in the room, Carole wouldn't have noticed an entire Pony Club wrapped in bath towels.

"Horse Wise, come to order!" Max called out.

"ALL RIGHT, THEN," Max said, wrapping up the meeting. "Who can name the five basic facial markings on a horse?"

Tiffani raised her hand and Max gave her a nod. "White face, stripe, blaze, snip, and star," she said.

"Very good. And how about the feet?"

Carole answered that one: "Long sock or stocking, short sock, white pastern, short white pastern, and coronet."

"Nice job," he said to both of them. It was a well-deserved compliment. For the entire meeting, which was on the subject of horse colors, every time Max had a question, either Carole or Tiffani had the answer for him. "So good, in fact, that I'd like to ask you two to do some research for us and present a report at the next unmounted meeting in two weeks. Would that be all right with you?"

"On what subject?" Tiffani asked.

"How about horse breeds?" Max suggested.

"Great!" Carole said. Then she turned to Tiffani. "I've got this terrific book. You're going to love it. But you probably already have it."

"If I do, it's in Tennessee," Tiffani said.

"Well, then we'll share. First, you can look up—"

"Ahem," Max said, cutting off their conversation. "I think I'm the one talking now. . . ."

"Sorry, Max," Carole said.

"The meeting is adjourned, but I do have a treat for you at the class, so hurry up, eat your lunches and get tacked up. We'll meet in the ring in one hour."

That gave the Pony Clubbers just enough time to gobble down sandwiches and tack up. Carole, however, was in no rush to eat. She wanted to talk to Tiffani some more, and she wanted to meet her horse.

"Why, of course you can meet Diamond," Tiffani told Carole. "He's the sweetest old boy in the whole state—at least that was true in Tennessee. I can't vouch for Virginia yet, but I'm pretty sure—"

"Don't say that until you meet Starlight," Carole said, teasing back.

"Is that the beautiful part-Thoroughbred bay with that pretty star on his face over there?" she asked.

"That's my boy," said Carole, flattered that Tiffani had

noticed her horse in the confusion of her first day at a new stable.

"And who owns the part Saddlebred that's in the stall across from Diamond?" Tiffani asked.

"That would be Belle. She belongs to Stevie Lake. Stevie's the one who—"

"I know Stevie," said Tiffani. "She came to my rescue and did most of the work cleaning out the trough this morning. She's lucky to have such a nice horse. You know, Saddlebreds and Tennessee walkers have a lot in common. They're both real American breeds, and they're practically cousins. I bet Belle and Diamond will get along like a house afire."

"Belle's a great horse," Carole told her. "She's kind of mischievous and she's got a mind of her own—just like Stevie, if you want to know the truth—but she's a joy to ride and Stevie's just crazy about her."

"No wonder," said Tiffani.

As the two of them walked together down the aisle, Carole took the opportunity to introduce Tiffani to all the horses there. Since the other riders were eating lunch, the girls had the stable to themselves, which allowed them to talk about horses without interruption. As they chatted, Carole became more and more aware that Tiffani really knew a great deal about horses. And she was a good listener, too. When they came to Belle's stall, Carole gave the mare a pat on her pretty face and formally introduced her to Tiffani.

14

"We've already met," said Tiffani, reaching to scratch Belle on the cheek just where she liked it best, instinctively knowing where it was. "And now I can introduce you to Diamond."

They turned around. Diamond was poking his head over the gate to his stall. In spite of the obvious joke about Tiffani's horse being named Diamond, it was clear he'd been given his name not for that but for the diamond-shaped star on his forehead.

The horse was tall, perhaps sixteen hands; his eyes glimmered intelligently in the sunlight that filtered into the stable. He greeted his owner with apparent affection, happily nibbling on the carrot she offered him.

"I missed him so while he was still at home," Tiffani said. "And this afternoon will be the first time I get to ride him. I haven't even unpacked his tack yet." She gestured toward a trunk outside the stall.

Carole leaned over and snapped open the latch on the trunk, lifting the lid. The trunk was neatly packed with everything a horse needed to travel. She reached in to pull out the saddle so that she could perch it on the nearby rack until Tiffani was ready to tack up.

"Huh?" Carole said, surprised, when her arm hit something funny as she tugged at the saddle. "What's this?"

When she looked again she knew what Max's surprise was. Diamond's saddle had a big padded hook on its left side. That was a rest for the rider's right leg. Tiffani rode her Tennessee walking horse sidesaddle!

"Now, EVERYBODY WATCH how she mounts," Max said
to the class a little later when Tiffani was beginning her
demonstration. "In many ways, riding sidesaddle is just
like riding astride. . . ."

Few people were actually hearing what Max said.
Carole, for one, was far too intent on not missing anything about Tiffani's technique. Her mind was flooded
with a hundred questions she hadn't had time to ask
during the lunch break, in addition to the three hundred she *had* asked during lunch break. Well, maybe not
three hundred, she consoled herself, but an awful lot.

Stevie wasn't thinking of questions right then. She
was thinking about answers. She nudged Lisa. "Well,
that explains the pink jodhpurs," she whispered.

Lisa didn't appear to have heard her. "I said, that explains the pink jodhpurs," Stevie repeated.

Lisa nodded absently, barely absorbing Stevie's words, and that annoyed Stevie a little more than she wanted to admit. She and Lisa had missed Carole at lunch. Stevie thought they really needed to get together to talk about the silliness of this new phenomenon that had hit Pine Hollow so hard: the Tiffani phenomenon. Between pink jodhpurs, li'l ole S'uthe'n expressions, and now sidesaddle riding, Stevie had had her fill of Miss Tiffani Thomas and thought it was high time for a Saddle Club meeting to talk about her.

"How about TD's after our class?" Stevie whispered, once again trying to get Lisa's attention. TD's—short for Tastee Delight—was an ice cream parlor within easy walking distance of the stable. The threesome often gathered there for Saddle Club meetings.

"Huh?"

"TD's?"

"Oh, sure," Lisa agreed.

One down. Now Stevie had to get Carole's attention. It wasn't easy. All the riders were on their horses, in a circle, facing the center of the ring where Tiffani was demonstrating sidesaddle technique.

"It's not really very different from riding astride in most ways," she said. "The horse—well, my li'l Diamond, anyway—seems to know to adjust to one-sided leg aids. I sometimes ride him astride just to see if he remembers, and, like an elephant, this ole boy never forgets!"

There was appreciative laughter from the other students.

"Well, class, it's not so different from a horse that can be trained in both English and Western, is it?" Max asked.

"And like a horse that responds to the different signals he might get from a rider or from a driver of a cart or wagon," Carole said.

"Exactly," Max agreed.

Stevie knew it wasn't going to be easy getting Carole's attention. When she got totally drawn into a subject—any subject, but especially one having to do with horses—it was hard to distract her.

Stevie raised her hand to wave at Carole. Carole didn't see her, but Max did.

"Stevie? You have a question?"

"Um, nothing," she said.

Tiffani continued. "I think the only thing that's hard at all for my li'l genius here is that I balance differently when I'm riding astride from the way I do when I'm in my sidesaddle. He's more used to the sidesaddle, so if I change to riding astride, it takes him a few minutes to become accustomed."

"Isn't it kind of dangerous?" Meg asked. "I mean, like, don't you fall off a lot?"

"No more than you do," Tifffani answered. "Actually, maybe less. This here leg rest will really hold you on the saddle tightly, so even at a pretty high jump—"

"You jump sidesaddle?" April blurted out.

"Well, sure," Tiffani told her. "You can do anything in a sidesaddle!"

"Psssst!" Stevie tried hissing to get Carole's attention. No luck.

"Whoooaaa," Tiffani said when Diamond shied a little. The horse settled immediately. Stevie hadn't even noticed because she was so intent on getting Carole's attention.

If Carole didn't notice a wave and she didn't hear a hiss, maybe she'd notice if Stevie did both at once.

"Psssssssssst!" Stevie hissed loudly, waving at the same time.

Carole didn't notice, but everyone else did—especially Diamond, who was more startled this time than he had been the first. He stepped to his left and gave an irritated buck, flicking his tail protectively as if he were moving out of the way of an attacking animal.

Tiffani, unprepared for that sudden movement, lurched to her left, and then, when Diamond stopped, she totally lost her balance and began to slip off the saddle, almost dangling from the leg rest. In balletic slow motion she recovered, first by grabbing the saddle and then by regaining her footing in the stirrup and pushing herself back up. She seemed to swerve to the right and then corrected her balance, regaining her position.

"Diamond!" she said, speaking firmly to her misbehaving mount.

"Stevie!" Max cried, speaking firmly to his misbehaving student once he was sure that Tiffani and Diamond were all right. They were a little shaken but fine.

"Max?" Stevie responded, as surprised as anyone at Diamond's reaction.

"Stevie, you know better than to make rapid, irritating motions and sounds around a horse, especially one in an unfamiliar setting. You owe Tiffani and Diamond an apology."

"I'm really sorry," Stevie said, meaning it. "I had no idea. I just wasn't thinking."

"Well, you should have been," Max said firmly. "And now you are excused from class. That should give you adequate time to think about the consequences the next time you do something like that, or in case someone else might ever do something that thoughtless to you."

She deserved it. She knew it. It had been stupid and thoughtless. Worse, it had been dangerous. It wasn't as if Carole was going to go anyplace other than TD's after class. They almost always went to TD's after class. Stevie didn't have to tie it down right then and there. What had she been thinking?

"I'm sorry, Max," she said, turning Belle to go into the barn. She was embarrassed and ashamed. It wasn't as if she'd never made a mistake, nor as if she would never make another, but to be punished in front of Miss Pink Jodhpurs . . .

"Oh, Max, it wasn't anything, you know?"

Stevie looked up to see if she'd heard that right. She had. Tiffani continued.

"I know she didn't mean anything by it. And I'm fine, and Diamond is fine. I just never had a chance to tell you all that he's really afraid of snakes and any hissing sound—Well, who could know that? Stevie's been so nice to me. She cleaned out that dirty ole trough with me and then she introduced me to everyone. Why, it would practically break my heart, and Diamond's here, too, I'm sure, if she had to leave?"

Was Stevie hearing this right? Was Miss Pink Jodhpurs standing up for her when she roundly deserved to be punished?

"And there she is, riding that beautiful ole half Saddlebred, practically a cousin to Diamond. Why, I know he'd be just heartbroken if they left? Max?"

Apparently there was something about sentences that ended with questions that appealed to Max. He took a deep breath and then let it out in a sigh.

"Okay," he said. "Stevie, you may stay, and I won't punish you further because I know you know better. Right?"

"Right," she murmured, halting Belle and returning to the circle.

Tiffani went back to her demonstration, showing the students how to signal turns and gait changes in a sidesaddle. Stevie watched, and maybe she absorbed some of the information, but almost all of her mind was concentrated on the fact that she didn't belong there. She'd done something quite unforgivable and should have been punished for it. Worse than being punished was being forgiven—by Miss Pink Jodhpurs.

After Tiffani had demonstrated her skills to the class, she offered Diamond to anyone who wanted to try riding sidesaddle. Most of the class eagerly waved their hands and then took turns. The exceptions were Stevie and most of the boys. One boy, Adam Levine, declared his utter curiosity and tried it out. When he was done, he slid down off the saddle, saying that once was enough. That made everybody but Stevie laugh.

Stevie wasn't in a laughing mood.

Carole tried it next. Stevie watched as she mounted Diamond. It was just like Carole to have such an easy time of it. She seemed to have some magical intuition that showed her how to do everything there was to do with horses. As soon as she was settled in the saddle, she looked as if she'd been there all her life.

Carole took Diamond for a turn around the schooling ring. He responded to her commands almost as smoothly as he had to Tiffani's. She sat in the saddle without a tilt, a jilt, or a jog.

"Why, you're a natural at this, Carole!" Tiffani declared when Carole drew Diamond to a halt.

"Oh, I don't think so," Carole said, dismounting with almost as much grace as she had shown when she mounted. "It's so different, even when it's so similar. I liked it all right, and thank you for letting me try it, but I think I'll stick to Starlight and a regular English saddle."

It was a different story when it was Lisa's turn. She had trouble mounting, trouble balancing herself, and trouble giving appropriate signals to Diamond.

"What am I doing wrong?" she asked plaintively.

"Almost everything," Max answered solemnly. Everybody, including Lisa and Stevie, laughed at that.

"You should relax a little," Tiffani suggested. "I think you're so afraid of making mistakes that you're just about guaranteeing them."

Lisa's face was set in firm determination. "All right," she agreed. "I'll relax."

But she didn't, and Diamond knew it. So did everybody else. Lisa gave Diamond the signal to begin walking, and although he seemed a little confused, confirming to Lisa that she'd done it wrong, he stepped forward, beginning a slow, dignified walk. Lisa responded to the horse's natural movement. At first she'd been more perched on the saddle than sitting into it, but once Diamond was moving, she slid more comfortably into the leather, allowing the full weight of her right leg to rest on the saddle's hook.

"Good," said Max.

Lisa knew she was making progress. It took her longer to go around the ring than it had Carole, because she did the whole circle at a walk. Even though what she'd done had been awkward and even klutzy, Lisa knew she'd learned something along the way. It was a familiar and exciting feeling, the same feeling she got when she understood something a teacher said that others found confusing. It was why she liked learning anything so much. As she dismounted, sliding down onto the turf in the schooling ring, she made up her mind to do it again.

"That was great!" she said. "Can I do it again sometime?"

"You sure can," said Max. "In fact, all of you are welcome to try sidesaddle riding at almost any time. As you've no doubt noticed when you've been cleaning tack, Pine Hollow owns several sidesaddles. If one of them fits you and your pony or horse, you are welcome to try it. I'll be happy to give you instruction—"

"I'll help," Tiffani offered.

"And Tiffani will help," Max said.

"And I'll do it," said Lisa, mostly to herself. She was

determined to find a saddle that fit Prancer and her and to work on this new skill a lot more.

"Now that we've tried that, let's work on our most basic skills," Max announced. "In every kind of riding, the most important thing is . . ." He waited for the answer.

"Balance," the members of the class answered. Then, knowing what was coming, they all reluctantly took their feet out of their stirrups. Riding without stirrups was Max's favorite way of teaching balance.

Stevie crossed her stirrups over Belle's saddle and followed Max's instructions. She was used to this exercise, and she was good at it. Belle had such smooth gaits that Stevie didn't mind being without stirrups even at a trot. She also knew it was an extremely useful and effective exercise. She only wished they had more time to work with it.

Instead the class had been spent paying a lot of attention to Miss Pink Jodhpurs and her "li'l ole horse." Sure, she knew what she was doing, but what was the point? Nobody rode sidesaddle anymore. Why would anyone want to?

Stevie recognized the darkness of her own mood, but there seemed little she could do to lighten it up. The fact that the rest of the class was oohing and aahing at Tiffani's ability to ride sidesaddle without a stirrup didn't help at all.

25

The end of class couldn't come soon enough. Stevie couldn't wait to groom and water Belle and then escape to the peace, quiet, and privacy of TD's to talk with her friends. And when Max finally dismissed the class, Stevie was the first one out of the saddle and into the stable.

It didn't help that Diamond's stall was right across the aisle from Belle's. It also didn't help that Tiffani prattled on about how she just knew that Belle and Diamond were going to be best friends because they were practically cousins. She apparently never registered the silence from across the aisle indicating that Stevie didn't much want to talk to her.

Stevie finished grooming and watering Belle in record time that afternoon. She eagerly walked down the aisle to help Lisa and then Carole finish their barn chores. Very quickly, all three of them were done, and after a brief stop in the locker area, they were on their way to TD's.

The girls found that someone was in their favorite booth. That didn't help to raise Stevie's spirits. She was beginning to think that absolutely nothing was going right that day. However, ice cream in a different booth was better than no ice cream. The girls slid into the one opposite their favorite.

When the waitress stopped by to take their orders, Carole asked for a butterscotch sundae with vanilla ice cream. Lisa just wanted some frozen banana yogurt.

Stevie, as usual, was hungry. And she, as usual, ordered a combination that gave her friends the chills.

"Peppermint stick ice cream with bubble gum bits and marshmallow sauce. Oh, plus three cherries and some strawberry sprinkles."

"That's it?" the waitress asked. Stevie was well known for adding afterthoughts to her sundae orders. This time she refrained from asking for licorice chips or caramel walnuts.

"Well, some whipped cream, of course."

"Of course," the waitress echoed. She disappeared with no further comment.

Lisa took a sip of water. "I always hate it when Max makes us ride without stirrups," she said. "It reminds me of how far I have to go before I'm a really good rider!"

Stevie and Carole laughed.

"I'll make you a deal," Stevie said. "I'll ride for you without stirrups if you'll go with my mother to the mall. She's been grumbling about my wardrobe, using words like *disgrace* and *embarrassing*."

"Do you suppose that has anything to do with the shirt you're wearing now?" Carole asked.

"Why, this is my favorite!" Stevie said. "And it's barely broken in!"

Lisa and Carole chuckled, admiring the seven or eight small holes they could see on the front of Stevie's faded T-shirt. It *was* her favorite, though. On one side

27

was a picture of a gooey sundae. On the back it read: LIFE IS UNCERTAIN. EAT DESSERT FIRST.

It was a fine T-shirt to wear at the stable and even at TD's. It was okay at home, too. It wasn't so fine anyplace else, especially not at school.

"Well, let's just say that perhaps your mother has a point," Lisa said. "And of course I'll come shopping with you and your mother. It can't possibly be as painful as shopping with *my* mother!"

"No, I actually meant that you'd go shopping with my mother without me," Stevie said.

She was about to launch into a hastily planned scheme to make that possible when the waitress arrived with their orders. Stevie stared at her sundae. There was something unsettling about it, and it took her a second to figure it out. Pink, pink, pink, white fluff, red chips, more white fluff. It looked like a Valentine's Day treat. It also looked like Tiffani Thomas. What had she been thinking?

Dismayed, she picked up her spoon and began the task of eating it anyway.

But when the waitress stepped away and Stevie looked up to thank her, for the first time she took a look at the occupants of The Saddle Club's favorite booth. They were none other than Tiffani Thomas herself, with Adam Levine—the one boy in the class who had wanted to try out the sidesaddle.

It wasn't easy for Stevie to look at Tiffani, but it was

harder to look at Adam. He was totally entranced by Tiffani, gazing at her over his untouched dish of ice cream. He hung on every word that came out of her mouth, every sentence that sounded like a question.

Stevie leaned over and whispered to her friends, tilting her head in the direction of Tiffani and Adam. "I didn't know boys liked that stuff," she said. "You know, all pink and fuzzy."

Lisa's eyes rolled up to the ceiling.

"Why do you think he wanted to try the sidesaddle?" Carole asked. "He was trying to impress her."

"They love it," Lisa said.

"Not ones who have any sense," Stevie said. "I mean, I can't see Phil spending one second goggling at her the way Adam is." Stevie's boyfriend was Phil Marsten. He lived in a nearby town and had his own horse. He was a very good rider, but Stevie couldn't even imagine him trying out a sidesaddle.

"No," Carole agreed. "Not Phil."

ON MONDAY AFTER SCHOOL, Stevie climbed the stairs to her bedroom, carrying all her books and her good intentions. She dropped the books on the floor before plopping onto her comfortable bed.

Her school day had been pretty good. She'd gotten back a history paper with a B, and she'd taken a pre-algebra test that she thought she'd aced. That wasn't what made it a good day, though. It had been a good day because it had been Tiffani-free. Since Tiffani went to Willow Creek Junior High—which was where both Lisa and Carole went—Stevie was guaranteed to be without her for the entire school day.

Tiffani wasn't that bad, really, Stevie told herself. She wasn't mean or anything. She wasn't a schemer the way Veronica diAngelo was. She wasn't stupid or boorish or rude. She was just so . . . Stevie couldn't find the right word to describe her. *Pink* was all that came to mind, and it felt odd to describe a person that way. But in Tiffani's case it seemed to fit.

Stevie sighed contentedly and reached for her phone. After all, it had been almost twenty-four hours since she'd talked to either Lisa or Carole. That needed to be rectified.

She dialed Carole's number first. Nobody was home, which was odd because Carole usually got home before Stevie. Maybe she'd gone to Pine Hollow or something. Lisa would know.

She dialed Lisa's number. The line was busy. Fifteen minutes later it was still busy, and another fifteen after that it was *still* busy.

Grumbling, Stevie picked up her book bag. If there was nothing else to do, she might as well get some homework done. She opened her history textbook and flipped to the assigned pages about the Roman empire. As Caesar was crossing the Rubicon, the phone rang. It was Lisa.

"I just got off the computer," she said, explaining the busy signal. "I found a whole Web site devoted to sidesaddle riding!"

"Be still, my heart," Stevie said sarcastically. Either Lisa didn't hear or the humor was lost on her.

"Well, you know, I'm always interested in learning something new. I was terrible on Saturday when I was riding Diamond, but I'm sure I could get better if I worked at it. Anything to do with horses is interesting."

"I know what you mean," Stevie said, relenting. "I liked learning how to drive a cart and a sleigh—not that I want to do it all the time, but it was fun. And speaking of fun, I tried to call Carole earlier, but she wasn't home yet. Any idea what she's up to?"

"Yeah," Lisa said. "She's meeting Tiffani at the library to work on their report about horse breeds."

"Oh," Stevie said.

"I've got some science homework to get to," said Lisa. "I'll see you Wednesday at riding class, okay?"

"Okay," Stevie said. She hung up the phone and turned her attention back to Julius Caesar. Before his triumphal march through the streets of Rome, the phone rang again. This time it was Carole.

"You won't believe all the stuff we found," Carole bubbled. "I mean, we'd both brought the books we had at home, and then there was an even better one at the library. We learned all about coldbloods and warmbloods. Did you know that *coldblood* refers to the large workhorses like the Friesians and Clydesdales because they do so much work in the cold areas of the world, like Scandinavia and northern Europe? The warmbloods are mixes of coldbloods and horses from the hot areas of the world, like Arabians, and that's why warmbloods have both strength and endurance. And then there are horses like the ones native to Mongolia, which might be the original horse breeds from which all the other horses descended, and those horses have some vague striping on their legs that looks a lot like zebra stripes! Isn't this interesting? I wonder how much time Max will give us for our report. I couldn't believe how much of this stuff Tiffani already knew. We looked in our books, all right, but she knew most of it anyway. We made copies of lots and lots of pictures so we can make charts of all the major breed groups of horses and then of ponies. I'm always amazed at how much there is to know. Don't you just love learning something new?"

Carole didn't stop to take a breath. Stevie thought she might talk for hours on the subject of South American breeds alone. Carole was like that. She was famous among her friends for being able to give what they jokingly called twenty-five-cent answers to nickel questions. Stevie was used to that and in fact had often benefited from it. In this case, though, she was finding it a little hard to take. She'd also heard about as much as she wanted to hear about the joys of learning something new—especially when all that new knowledge was attached to Tiffani Thomas. This day wasn't turning out to be Tiffani-free after all.

"Hey, stop a second," Stevie said. "Save some surprises for me until you give your actual report."

"Oh, right, yeah," Carole said. "But there's so much. We won't be able to tell it all no matter how much time Max gives us."

"Well, whatever is left over, you can tell Lisa and me at our next sleepover."

"Deal," Carole said. "So what are you up to?"

"Julius Caesar," Stevie answered. "He's just come to power in Rome."

"I'll let you get back to it. I'll see you Wednesday."

"Bye," Stevie said. She returned her attention to Caesar's exploits. Somehow they seemed to make more sense to her than either of her friends.

ON TUESDAY AFTER school, Stevie was denied the luxury of escaping to her room. For some reason her mother was oblivious to the humor in Stevie's most recent practical joke on her beloved twin brother. It was just shaving cream!

The net result was that Stevie had to weed the flower bed in front of the house. And she'd been threatened with perpetual raking if she took out so much as one impatiens. If there was anything she hated more than weeding, it was raking. She was being very careful. She was paying so much attention to the flower bed that she hardly noticed when people walked by. But she couldn't miss Lisa in her riding clothes on her way back from Pine Hollow.

"Hi," Stevie greeted her. "How's Prancer?"

34

"Oh, I wasn't riding Prancer," Lisa said, almost breathless with excitement. "I tried all of Max's side-saddles on her, but none of them fit. It was okay, though, because, as usual, Tiffani was very generous. She let me ride Diamond. It was great. I didn't do anywhere near as many dumb things as I did when I tried on Saturday. All that reading yesterday really paid off. Tiffani could hardly believe how much better I was. That doesn't mean I was good or anything, but I wasn't so obviously a beginner. It's really fun, you know. You sit a whole different way on the horse, more balancing on your thigh than on your bottom, but it works, somehow. You should try it, Stevie."

"I did try it, you know," Stevie said.

"I didn't see you on Diamond."

"Not on Diamond. It was a while ago. It was okay, but frankly I'd just as soon stick to regular riding," Stevie said, yanking out an impatiens.

"There certainly is plenty more I need to learn about riding astride, so I'm not at all sure I ought to spend much time on the sidesaddle riding, but it was fun."

"How right you are," Stevie said, trying to stuff the bedraggled flower back into the earth. "Listen, I'll see you tomorrow, okay?"

"Okay, bye," said Lisa, and she continued on her way home.

*   *   *

CLASS ON WEDNESDAY wasn't much of an improvement. In the first place, Tiffani was there. She and Carole were buzzing together beforehand, talking about their presentation: Which one of them needed to buy oak tag and where could they meet to glue everything down and practice their speeches?

That surprised Stevie. The idea of Carole actually having to practice talking endlessly about horses was a bit much. She did that as naturally as she breathed.

Every time Tiffani did something in class, like change gaits or diagonals or make Diamond back up, Lisa would say something like, "Oh, that's how it's done sidesaddle!"

Even Max seemed a little overcome by the presence of Tiffani and her sidesaddle wonder horse. "You know, riders," he said, "this new aspect of riding has inspired me. I am going to give you all an assignment to work on by yourselves. I want each of you to learn something new. Pick something you haven't done before—or that you've done only a little of—something you've wanted to have a chance to learn more about, and teach it to yourself. I don't care what it is. Each of you is on your own to pick a topic and learn it. It can be a skill or a research report or anything at all. If you need help, you can get some from me or from your classmates, but the project should be yours alone. We can all share our new skills or information with one another at the Horse Wise meeting in two weeks."

It took Stevie exactly two and a half seconds to decide what her new skill would be. She would figure out a way to get a nice pair of new black cotton socks into Tiffani's laundry so that she'd never have to see those pink jodhpurs again. If she used her own blue bathrobe, it would be too obvious. Socks were good. They were really anonymous. Or a towel.

"Class dismissed!" Max announced.

Not soon enough, Stevie thought.

THURSDAY WILL BE OKAY, thought Stevie. First, no Tiffani at school. Then Carole was doing something with her father after school, so she wouldn't be able to meet with Tiffani and then tell Stevie all about it. And Lisa was going to the orthodontist with her mother, and that meant no Pine Hollow and no more breathless descriptions about sidesaddle riding. It would definitely be a Tiffani-free day.

After school, as soon as Stevie finished raking the side yard, she escaped to the relative quiet of her room and the exploits of Julius Caesar. Just as she was getting into the reading, the phone rang.

"Hi, is this Stevie?"

"Yes," Stevie said uncertainly. She wasn't uncertain that she was Stevie. She was just uncertain that she wanted to talk with the person who was calling.

"It's Tiffani!" the person announced.

"Hi," Stevie said.

"You know, I just had this wonderful idea?" There she was, asking questions again. "I was thinking about how my Tennessee walker and your Saddlebred are practically siblings, you know?"

"Well, sort of," Stevie agreed.

"And they just really seem to be getting along like a house afire?"

"Yes?" Stevie said, irritated that she, too, was asking a question but also hoping that Tiffani would get to her point.

"Well, I wondered if it wouldn't be fun if the two of them—and us, of course—could take a trail ride together tomorrow afternoon? I know Diamond would just love to get a chance to see some of the woods around his new home, and Max tells me that there's nobody who knows the trails better than you do, so it just seemed so utterly natural that we should go together with our horses?"

Stevie loved to take trail rides on Friday afternoons. It always seemed to make the point that the weekend was beginning. A trail ride was freedom, so different from school and the structure of weekdays, to say nothing of weeding and raking. It was a sort of TGIF release. But with Tiffani?

"Gee, I don't know, Tiffani," she said. "I've got a bunch of things I have to do, and I was sort of counting on the afternoon." Right, like her Christmas thank-you notes. Now that it was April, it was definitely time to get them done. And her mother had been nagging her about doing some shopping. And there was that dentist's appointment she'd been putting off. . . . "I just don't think I can," she said. "But you go ahead and have fun."

"Oh, too bad!" said Tiffani, clearly oblivious to Stevie's lukewarm response. "I was hoping to get more of a chance to know you. After all, you were so nice to me at the first meeting. I wanted a way to say thank you, too. But if you can't do it tomorrow, how about on Saturday after Horse Wise and after the class? We should be able to get in a little time together."

"Right, sure," Stevie said.

"Oh, goody," Tiffani responded. "I'll see you then!" And she hung up the phone.

Stevie sighed. Saturday was a long, long time away, wasn't it?

CAROLE AND LISA reached Pine Hollow early on Saturday morning. Carole decided to walk Barq on a lead to make sure his sore foot wasn't bothering him anymore. She had him in the ring when she saw a familiar car pull into the stable's parking lot. Phil Marsten stepped out and walked over to the fence.

"What are you doing here?" she asked.

"Well, my mother said something about devoting the day to the mall, and I reminded her that Willow Creek was on the way, so I thought I'd surprise Stevie and come to the Horse Wise meeting. Do you think she'll mind?"

"Mind? Are you crazy? She'll be thrilled. She's not here yet, so if you want to help, you can take Barq's lead. I want to watch him from across the ring. Judy said he should be healed by now, but I wanted to be certain."

Willingly Phil climbed through the fence and began walking the horse around the ring. A few minutes later, Tiffani Thomas came out of the barn leading her horse, and Carole introduced the new girl to Phil.

"Tiffani's staying with her aunt in Willow Creek for the semester," Carole explained. "She's just joined Horse Wise because her horse, Diamond, just arrived. Tiffani, this is Phil Marsten. He's a friend of Stevie's. He lives two towns over—or is it three?"

"It depends on which route you take," he explained. "Nice horse," he said, admiring Diamond's conformation. "Tennessee walker?"

"Why, you know as much about horses as Stevie and her friends here! You-all are just amazing?"

"Flattery will get you everywhere," Phil said. "Here, I think Barq is just fine. Would you like me to take Diamond for a walk so that you can stand back and watch?"

"Sure thing," Tiffani said, swapping lead lines with Phil. "Not that I think there's anything wrong with my darlin' here. It's just that it's been a couple of days since he's had any exercise, and since we're going on a trail ride after class, I wanted to be sure he'd be warmed up for it. I sure don't want him to stiffen?"

"Good idea," Phil agreed. He walked the horse for another ten minutes while Carole, Lisa, and Tiffani finished getting ready for the meeting.

STEVIE WAS TORN. It sometimes happened that something she was excited and happy about was going to occur on a day when there was something she was also unhappy about. Like a dentist's appointment on the same day as a party. In this case, the problem was that Saturday meant both Horse Wise and the trail ride with Tiffani.

It took her fifteen minutes instead of the usual five to find a matching pair of socks, and she had to dig all the way through her laundry pile (sometimes also referred to as her closet) to find the shirt she wanted to wear. And then it took another five minutes to locate her riding hat, although it was on the shelf where she always put it.

Stevie just wasn't as enthusiastic this Saturday morning as she usually was.

When she got to Pine Hollow, the meeting was about to begin. She felt a little guilty that she hadn't gotten there in time to give Belle a grooming and a treat, but she'd have time before class. She smiled and waved at the familiar faces and then looked for Carole and Lisa.

There they were—and sitting right next to them was Phil! Stevie smiled broadly and waved eagerly as she made her way through the seated Pony Club members to join her friends.

That Phil was there was good news any day, but today it was A-1, perfect, wonderful, terrific, great news. As long as her boyfriend was making a surprise visit, anyone, even Tiffani, would understand why she just had to cancel the trail ride.

With a warm, happy feeling, Stevie settled down onto the floor of Max's office just as Max called the meeting to order.

This was a mounted meeting, which meant that soon most or all of the members would be on their ponies and horses. Max wanted everyone to gather in his office first for announcements. His main announcement was actually more of a question.

"I'd like to know, if you can tell me, what each of you has decided to take up in our Learn Something New project. I'm asking this question primarily because I will need to know if you need any extra equipment or a special setup next week for your demonstrations. The other reason I'm asking, of course, is that I'm curious."

The riders laughed at his honesty. Max looked around the room for someone to volunteer.

"I'm trying to learn something about sidesaddle riding," said Jessica, one of the younger riders.

"Me too," said another.

Lisa nodded as if in agreement.

It didn't surprise Stevie that that was Lisa's project.

Lisa had been excited on Tuesday after she'd ridden Diamond. And then she'd talked about the Web site.

It did surprise Stevie, however, that Tiffani had inspired about a quarter of the riders to take up sidesaddle riding. Maybe that was just because it wasn't all that hard. If you were going to learn something new, it might as well be something easy.

"Cart driving," said another rider. Two other members raised their hands on that, too.

"Bareback riding," said Meg.

"Good for balance," Max said approvingly. "But don't forget your riding helmet."

"I promise."

"Research on the Bureau of Land Management," said Joe Novick, referring to the care the government gives to horses and burros living in the wild on federal land in the West.

"Good," Max said.

"Polo," said Veronica. There were a few snickers. Although polo was a very rugged sport that required excellent horsemanship and athletic skills, it was usually reserved for the extremely wealthy—people who could afford to own a lot of ponies. Although Veronica was very wealthy, she wasn't *that* wealthy, but she clearly wanted to be.

"I think she means Ralph Lauren," Phil whispered to Stevie. That made Stevie smile. Veronica was definitely fashion-conscious.

"Carole and Tiffani, I guess your horse breed report will qualify as something new, right?" Max asked.

"That's what we were hoping you'd say," said Carole. Carole was never one to avoid learning about horses, but the time for one project was all she could devote outside her schoolwork.

Max looked at Stevie then. Stevie had been so interested in everybody else's projects that she'd hardly had time to notice that she didn't have one of her own. Even if she was still working on the black-socks-in-the-laundry prank, and even though she was pretty sure Max would welcome the end of the pink jodhpurs, she wasn't convinced that he would think that qualified as learning something new.

Stevie cast her eyes to the dust on her riding boots. Max didn't say anything else.

"Okay, now, let's all get tacked up. We're going to work on very specific skills today: We're going to play games!"

There was a general round of applause. Mounted games were pure fun for everybody. Stevie decided that although the day had begun with a giant cloud over it, everything was turning out rosy. Phil was there, she didn't have to go on a trail ride with Tiffani, and now she'd even have a chance to beat Phil at games.

Max had a long list of games for the meeting, and he even let the games run over into the class time, since everybody seemed to be having so much fun. The only cloud came when Tiffani had difficulty picking up a flag on the right side. Leaning over so far made her lose her balance, and she tumbled out of her sidesaddle.

Stevie didn't mind that part at all because Tiffani wasn't hurt in the least and it got a gigantic mud smear on her usually clean jodhpurs. What did bother Stevie was that almost everybody else in the class immediately rode over to help her.

"Are you all right?"

"Did you hurt yourself?"

"Are you cut anywhere?"

"Ooooooh, that must hurt!"

All that sympathy for one little fall seemed more than excessive.

Tiffani seemed to think so, too, and simply said, "I'm fine," and climbed back into the saddle as quickly as she could. She was embarrassed, as, Stevie thought, she should be. Nobody should fall out of the saddle doing something so simple!

Finally, after the meeting turned into class and after the class was over, Max dismissed the riders. It was time for a late lunch—fortunately Phil was prepared for that—and then . . .

"Well," Tiffani declared, placing her sandwich neatly on the napkin she'd laid out on the ground in front her. "We should be able to start our trail ride in about an hour. That's a nice time, because it'll give my Diamond and his cousin Belle a chance to rest before we go off into the woods."

"Well, gee, Tiffani," Stevie began, smiling at Phil. "You know Phil is here for the whole afternoon—"

"I know, he told me while he was walking Diamond for me this morning. Isn't that just great?"

"Sure, but I guess that means we can't have our trail ride."

"Why, didn't he tell you? He's comin' along! And I was so sorry that you hadn't had a chance to invite Carole and Lisa along with us, so I just took the bull by the horns—or should I say, the horse by the mane—and told them it wouldn't be the same without them. Right?"

"Right," Lisa agreed. "And Max told me I should ride Comanche because he knows one of the side-saddles fits him, so I can try that out on the trail. What do you think of that?"

For the second time that day, Stevie didn't have an answer to a question.

6

IT WOULD BE HARD to stay disagreeable, Stevie thought.
Although she was on a trail ride with Tiffani, who was
all sidesaddled up and everything, she also had her
three favorite people in the whole wide world right
there with her. Carole, Lisa, and Phil would be plenty
of cushioning against anything Tiffani had to dish out
to her.

"Oh, Stevie, Belle is such a lovely horse!" Tiffani
said.

Stevie smiled and nodded. There was hardly any way
to disagree with that. "And Diamond is, too," Stevie
told her. Her mother had instilled good manners far too
deeply in Stevie for her not to feel obliged to return the
compliment.

"Say, Stevie, what are you doing for Learn Something New?" Lisa asked.

That seemed like a pretty neutral topic, but of course Lisa didn't know about the sock plan. Before Stevie could answer, Carole added, "I was thinking you might do something about reining."

"Maybe," Stevie said noncommittally.

"Well, I'm planning some historical research," said Lisa, clucking her tongue so that Comanche, who seemed slightly nonresponsive to one-sided aids, would keep up with the other riders while they crossed the field. The trails were in the woods on the other side.

"I thought you were studying sidesaddle riding," said Stevie, nodding to the tack on Comanche.

"Oh, no, that's just to try something out. I don't really think of it as learning something new. I wanted to study up on some of the things that Carole's talked about—the history of horses in the military and the influence that has had on the way we ride today."

"Even down to mounting the horse on the left," said Carole.

"How's that?" Lisa asked.

"Oh, I know about that," said Tiffani.

"Well, tell us," Phil said. "I'm interested."

"Just imagine you're a soldier," said Tiffani. "I mean, not that that's so hard to imagine, you being so big and all that."

Stevie gagged. Nobody noticed.

"Since you're going to use your right hand to hold your sword, you have to wear it on your left side, or else you would never get it out of the scabbard. So, there it is, hanging down your left leg, and it would be the biggest ole nuisance in the world to get it up and over the horse if you were mounting from the right, so the soldiers mounted from the left."

"Why, I never would have thought of that," said Phil. "You certainly know an awful lot about horses and riding!"

Stevie gagged again.

"Are you okay, Stevie?" Tiffani asked.

"I'm fine," Stevie muttered, holding Belle's reins a little tighter to slow the mare down. She didn't really need to be so close to Tiffani, and if her friends, most especially her boyfriend, were going to be so gushy over Miss Pink Jodhpurs, Stevie wasn't at all sure she needed to be anywhere close to any of them.

It didn't work, however. Tiffani turned to her as they approached the woods. "Now, tell me, Stevie, which one of these trails should we try first?"

Stevie sighed. She was stuck and she knew it. Just as she was too polite to ignore a compliment, she was too nice to upset an afternoon for her friends. They seemed to be having an easier time than she was at being nice to Tiffani, but in spite of the frilly pink, fuzzy-sweatered, lace-ornamented newcomer, Stevie was on a

trail ride, and when it came to trail rides, she always
had definite ideas.

"To the creek, of course," she said. Carole, Lisa, and
Phil nodded in agreement, and the horses all walked
along jauntily.

Most of the trail was narrow, and the riders had to go
in single file and at a walk. Carole took the lead. Lisa
was behind her, followed by Tiffani and then Phil.
Stevie was at the rear. That suited her just fine. Nobody would expect to hear from her, and she could almost be by herself.

Words and phrases drifted back to her.

Lisa asked for help and advice on her sidesaddle. Tiffani was only too happy to provide it. Carole asked her
for information about breeds for their all-important report, due the following week.

Then, to Lisa's delight, Phil began asking Tiffani
more questions about military riding. It turned out that
this was another one of those areas where Tiffani knew
a great deal. Lisa's report was well under way.

"Hey, Stevie, you okay back there?" Tiffani asked,
looking over her shoulder.

"Fit as a fiddle," said Stevie, wondering vaguely
where she had ever come up with such a fatuous phrase.

"Oh, Stevie, you're so funny!" Tiffani responded.

Stevie rolled her eyes.

"Say, Phil, do you have any idea how lucky you are
to have a wonderful girlfriend like Stevie?" Tiffani

asked. "I just don't know how I would have made it through my first day at Pine Hollow without her. I mean, not that Pine Hollow is a hard place to be or anything, but Stevie just made me feel so welcome from the very first minute I saw her that I knew I was right at home?"

"Oh, she's a great girl, all right," Phil agreed.

"Better than great," said Tiffani.

"Yes, better," said Phil.

"And then for her to agree to show me the trails in the woods! Why, it was a whole 'nother nice thing for sweet Stevie to do."

"Definitely sweet," said Phil. "And speaking of sweet, I'm really curious about how you got to riding sidesaddle in the first place and what it's like and how you trained Diamond there?"

Did Stevie's ears deceive her or was her very normal Phil beginning to talk like Tiffani? Had he actually just ended a sentence that wasn't a question with a question mark?

"Oh, yes, do tell," Carole said eagerly. "I've been meaning to ask you."

It turned out to be a long story, something involving one of Tiffani's first instructors who'd had a sore right foot. Stevie wasn't very interested in the question, and she was certainly not interested in the answer. She turned her attention inward, because she was afraid if she didn't, she would either blow up or throw up, and neither seemed likely to please her companions at this point.

Who did Phil think he was, talking with Tiffani about Stevie as if she weren't there? And having to be reminded that Stevie was more than great! As long as she'd known him, he'd never told her she was "sweet," as in "sweet li'l ole Stevie." Why did he have to be discussing that now, with someone who was almost a stranger? Tiffani was flirting—with Phil!

Now that they'd been on the trail for twenty minutes, it wasn't as hard to be disagreeable as it had been when they'd first started out. Stevie found that she was no longer seeing pink—she was starting to see red.

Every time Tiffani opened her mouth, she batted her eyes, smiling, flattering, and flirting—with Stevie's boyfriend.

And the worst part was that Phil didn't seem to mind a bit.

Stevie rode in silence, unwilling to make a scene, uncertain what mattered and what didn't. She barely noticed the trees, the plants, the birds, the soft forest floor. She almost didn't even notice when Belle started to nibble at some weeds—the kind that would make her very sick.

"Stevie!" Lisa called back.

Stevie tugged at her reins. Belle lifted her head and continued walking.

53

When they got to the creek, everybody dismounted. It was too cool to go wading, but it wasn't too cool to sit on the rock and chat. Stevie sat with her friends, but if someone had asked her later what they had talked about, she wouldn't have had the vaguest idea. It was a blur. All she saw was Tiffani, smiling at Phil, blinking sweetly, teasing, putting her hand on his arm. "Oh, Phil!" Tiffani exclaimed. And Stevie saw Phil smiling back, blinking back, and never once moving his arm out of Tiffani's reach.

He likes it, he likes it, he likes it. The words coursed through Stevie's mind like a poison.

"We ought to be heading back about now," Carole said in her usual businesslike manner. "After all, the horses have been working for a while, what with all the games and then the lesson and now the trail ride. They must be as ready for some rest as we are—not that I'm really tired."

"You're never tired," said Lisa. "But I'm getting that way now. I think it must be the sidesaddle. Do you get more tired sidesaddle than astride?" she asked Tiffani.

"Oh no, but I'm used to it. It's like my muscles just know?"

"I guess mine haven't graduated from school yet," said Lisa. Tiffani must have thought that was awfully funny, because it made her laugh very hard, almost as hard as she laughed when she realized how much trouble she and Lisa were going to have remounting without a mounting block.

Fortunately Phil was there to help them. It was almost more than Stevie could bear, watching her boyfriend lift Tiffani Thomas into the saddle.

Stevie led the way back to the stable at the fastest safe speed she and Belle could manage.

STEVIE'S HEAD WAS SPINNING. She couldn't believe how totally unhappy she was. She was angry with her friends, furious at Phil, and inconsolable about Tiffani.

Stevie knew herself pretty well, and she knew that although she was more than capable of being annoyed by annoying people, this went well beyond that. She even understood that it wasn't totally rational. There was something about Tiffani that irked her more than she could say, and every time someone she liked didn't feel the same way, she got irked at them, too. When that included the three people she cared the most about in the world, she was in trouble.

She had to find a way out, a solution, a resolution. She thought about all these things as she groomed Belle, totally ignoring, insofar as she could, the buzz of activity across the hall. Riders stopped by to admire Diamond and to ask Tiffani about sidesaddle riding.

Was that what bothered her? Stevie asked herself. Was it because Tiffani was getting a lot of attention? Stevie liked attention, but she never begrudged it to anyone else who deserved it, and she could genuinely understand that people were curious about Tiffani and Diamond. Also, there was no question that Tiffani was someone who genuinely cared about other people. She'd learned absolutely everyone's name in a day and had a knack for recalling horses' names and details— "Why, I never saw anyone jump so smoothly as you did on Comanche. Was that really the first time you'd ridden him, Amy?"

And the pink and frills? Stevie shrugged. What a rider wore was no more important than the color of the horse she rode. It meant nothing.

So why did these things irk her? It was sort of like she'd been taken over by some kind of demon, and when it came to how Tiffani and Phil got along, the demon had a specific name: jealousy. But how on earth could Stevie be jealous? Phil was way too smart to fall for pink and frills, and she knew Phil too well to think his flirting with Tiffani meant anything. What mattered was how Stevie and Phil felt about one another, not about how Tiffani flirted or how Phil flirted back.

The only way to rout out a demon like jealousy was to bring it out in the open, talk about it, understand it.

Once it was understood, it couldn't possibly have any meaning. That was the answer. The one thing that would really make Stevie feel better was to spend some time with Phil.

It turned out to be easy to arrange that. There had been a lot of talk about TD's as their trail ride had come to an end. Carole and Lisa were eager to spend more time talking with Tiffani—the repository of all horse information in the world, Stevie grumbled to herself, momentarily forgetting her resolve—about their research projects. This would not be good for Stevie and she knew it. She was saved from disaster by her own white knight. While she was stammering and trying to come up with a reasonable excuse, Phil supplied her with one.

"I just can't today," he said. "Much as I would like a sundae and some good horse talk, my mother is picking me up at Stevie's place at four o'clock. That doesn't give us time to eat a sundae, even in a hurry." Then he turned to Stevie. "You can go with them if you'd like—" he began.

"No thanks," she said hastily. "I'll walk back to my place with you."

"Okay," he said. And the deal was made.

When Stevie finished tending to Belle, she put her tack away and went to look for Phil, expecting to find him in the locker area or chatting with Max or Red as he usually did. No such luck. He was among the group in the hallway watching Tiffani groom Diamond as if they'd never witnessed a grooming before. Tiffani was willingly answering questions about her Tennessee walking horse and about sidesaddle riding.

"It's a real American breed," she said. "Just as much as the Saddlebred, like Belle there, though Belle is a Saddlebred mix and Diamond is a purebred walker."

Phil nodded.

What Tiffani had said was absolutely, one hundred percent true, but it irked Stevie the same way that everything the girl said, especially when Phil agreed with it, irked her. It was definitely time to go.

She tugged on Phil's sleeve. "I'm ready," she told him.

"Me too," he said, taking her hand.

They left the stable together and began the walk home. It wasn't a long walk, but Stevie was hopeful it would be long enough for them to really enjoy one another's company in a pleasant, Tiffani-free atmosphere that would set her mind at ease.

"I'm glad the weather was nice for the trail ride," Stevie said, knowing that weather was considered the most neutral topic of all.

"Oh, yes," said Phil. "It would have been a shame if Tiffani's introduction to the Pine Hollow trails had been marred by rain or worse."

That was not the response Stevie was hoping for.

"Not that rain is all that bad," Stevie said.

"Oh, but it would have damaged that pretty sweater she was wearing," said Phil.

Definitely not the response Stevie was hoping for.

"Sort of an odd outfit for a day of horses, didn't you think—all that pink?"

Phil shrugged. "I don't know. It just seems to suit some girls, you know. I mean, that girl was born to wear lace." Phil seemed to sense that he'd crossed a line. "Not all girls, of course. I mean, I have trouble seeing you in pink and lace. It's like it's too girly for you, you know?"

Things were not going the way Stevie had hoped. What was wrong with pink? What made Phil think she couldn't wear pink things? And lace? And an angora sweater? She could do that. She knew she could. *Why would he think I couldn't?* she wondered. *Tiffani doesn't have a patent on pink! Anyone is allowed to wear it—even me.*

"The sidesaddle riding is really interesting," said Phil. "Not that I want to do it, but frankly I'd be interested in trying it because it's so different. You know, there's something lovely and graceful about the lines of a sidesaddle rider."

"Lines?"

"Sure, the way she looks in the saddle. It's elegant

and charming and, in an old-fashioned way, very feminine. I can see Scarlett O'Hara riding around Tara. . . ."

Feminine, elegant, charming. Those were nice words from Phil, words Stevie didn't ever recall hearing him utter about her. Visions of Rhett Butler popped into Stevie's head. She did her best to shove them back out again. Phil with a pencil mustache was more than she could handle right then.

She was spared further visions when the first of a barrage of spitballs hit her. She didn't know where they were coming from, but she had no doubt who was propelling them.

"Alexander Lake!" she said. "You come out of there!"

Alex did. He stood up from behind a bush in front of the Lakes' house (in a bed of flowers that Stevie had weeded on Tuesday), pointed his straw at Stevie, and let fly with another spitball, dart-gun style. This one hit Phil.

"What's this about?" Phil asked.

"It all has to do with some shaving cream," Stevie said, offering no further explanation. None was needed. Phil was aware of the ongoing practical-joke battles that Stevie had with her brothers, most especially with her twin. Phil had two sisters whom he found almost as annoying as Stevie found her three brothers. He was always sympathetic, and often inspired, by Stevie's sibling rivalries. Being hit by a spitball helped spur his sympathies, too.

"I'll get the hose," he offered.

Stevie nodded, but she was more interested in direct retaliation. She dived at her brother, startling him into dropping his straw and spitballs. The two of them scrambled in the freshly weeded dirt of the flower bed, punching and slapping one another. Nobody was getting seriously hurt. That was never the intention, but annoyance had its limits, and Stevie simply had to stop Alex.

The whole thing came to an abrupt halt when Phil turned on the water and began to spray both of them. At that moment, Stevie was lying on the ground and Alex was standing over her in triumph, a foot on her chest, as if he'd just discovered a new land and was about to plant a flag in her.

Stevie was the first to crack. With her brother standing above her and water raining over her, there was nothing to do but laugh. The jouncing of her chest when she started to guffaw upset Alex's balance, and the next thing Stevie knew, Alex was sitting next to her in the wet grass beside the flower bed, laughing every bit as hard as she was. By the time Phil returned from putting the hose away, Alex and Stevie were shaking hands and forgiving one another, a little.

Alex stood up. "Listen, I've got to go now. But don't

get any more bright ideas about whipped cream labels on shaving cream cans, okay?"

"Deal," said Stevie. She took Phil's proffered hand and got to her feet. "Thanks for spraying Alex," she said. "You really got him."

"He wasn't who I was trying to get," Phil said. "I was trying to get both of you because I knew it was the only way to break up the fight before your mother got wind of it. I don't like the idea of you being grounded until you're twenty-five. Think of this as enlightened self-interest. Come on. Let's get you dried off, okay?"

"Okay," she said, leading the way into the house. Stevie grabbed a towel from the laundry room and the two of them headed into the family room in the basement, where they might have a little peace and quiet. Alex was gone, Chad was at soccer practice, and Michael was at a friend's house.

While Stevie toweled her hair dry, Phil put their favorite CD on the stereo. Then she handed him a Ping-Pong paddle. By the time they began playing, everything seemed very normal to her. There was no talk of pink, no discussion about sidesaddle riding. There was simply their own brand of competitive Ping-Pong. And Phil won. Stevie thought that perhaps one of his serves was actually on the white line, but somehow it seemed right to let him feel like the victor, the stronger, the Man.

When they were done with that, they played video

games. Stevie was off her game that afternoon. Phil was ahead by 27,000 life points by the time they heard the doorbell ring at exactly four o'clock.

"I guess I'd better go," he said, standing up and taking her hand.

"I guess," she agreed, standing and facing him.

Phil swept a lock of hair back from her face and gave her a quick but very sweet kiss. Then he held her at arm's length and smiled, just looking at her. It made Stevie feel very beautiful. She practically floated up the basement steps to open the door for Mrs. Marsten.

"Hi, Ste—Is that you, Stevie?" Mrs. Marsten greeted her.

"Hello, Mrs. Marsten," Stevie responded. "I hope we didn't keep you waiting. We were just down in the basement playing video games."

"Of course," Mrs. Marsten said almost as if she didn't believe Stevie. Then Phil said good-bye and was out the door. Stevie waved at him through the screen door as the car backed out of her driveway.

Just before she pulled out onto the street, Mrs. Marsten gave Stevie one more very curious look. Then she turned the wheel and took Phil home.

What was that about? Stevie wondered. She shrugged. Sometimes other kids' parents could be funny, and there was no explaining it, though Mrs. Marsten was usually almost as normal as Stevie's own parents. Shrugging again, Stevie went back downstairs and put away the video games, definitely interested in erasing Phil's 27,000 life points before one of her brothers found out how badly she'd played, and then she went back up to her own room. She hadn't even had a chance to shower after her ride. She was ready to freshen up.

She picked up her bathrobe and went into the bathroom. There a very strange image greeted her from the mirror. It was Stevie, probably, but she was barely recognizable through the streaks of mud on her face and hair.

"Oh no," she said, stepping back from the mirror. And that was when she could see Alex's very large, muddy footprint across her chest.

"Oh no!"

8

"HEY! I FOUND A PICTURE of a mustang, and here's one of a palomino, so I think that covers all the breeds descended from the ponies left in North America by the Spanish *conquistadores*, right?" Carole said, eagerly picking up her scissors to clip the photographs from a magazine.

After the trip to TD's, Tiffani, Lisa, and Carole had all gone to the Willow Creek library to work on their projects. The library had a workroom where students could talk to one another. It was the perfect place to work on projects, with its big tables and large sunny windows. Lisa was at one end of the table, a stack of books on horsemanship and history in front of her. She was looking up everything she could find about the military history of horses.

Carole and Tiffani had brought most of their own materials. Carole had brought a selection of what she called her favorite horse magazines. That had made even Tiffani laugh, because Carole didn't have a "favorite" horse magazine. Any horse magazine was her favorite, and the size of her stack proved that. It must have weighed twenty pounds and had filled her backpack.

Carole had shrugged off her friends' laughter. It was working, wasn't it? She'd found pictures of every breed so far, and Tiffani seemed only too happy to paste them down on the charts they were making for their presentation.

"Oh, and here's another color pattern for the Appaloosa," Carole announced, clipping busily.

"All right, then next come the ponies," said Tiffani, pulling another chart out of the stack. "I think this is the last of them." She riffled through the stack. "Yes, it is, unless we actually manage to find a picture of the Mongolian wild horse."

"It's okay," Carole said. "I think I can draw one. It may not be perfect, but since I doubt anybody in Horse Wise has ever seen one, nobody's going to be too fussy. Boy, I hope I get the leg stripes right. Maybe I should see if I can find a picture of a zebra. And here are the pony pictures. I cut them out last night when I came across a whole series of articles on them. I've got most of the American breeds and the ones from the British

Isles, plus Icelandic, and that gray French breed—
Camargue, is it?"

"Yup," Tiffani said, taking the stack of photographs
from Carole. "Wow, thanks." She pasted the collection
of pony pictures on the chart while Carole went to talk
to the librarian. "And how are you doing?" Tiffani
asked Lisa.

"Just fine," Lisa said. "I'm learning a lot. I knew that
dressage descended from military techniques, but I
didn't realize how much."

"Oh, absolutely," Tiffani said. "Right down to the
fact that most of the signals are given with subtle leg
movements. That way the soldier had his arms free for
battle."

Lisa made a note.

"And there are other customs that have come down
to us from military riders as well."

"Like?"

"Well, like the side of the road we drive on. I'm not
sure exactly how this worked, but I've been told that it
was considered a friendly gesture to ride to the right
when someone was riding toward you. That way, if you
happened to have a sword in your hand, it would be
very hard to attack because the sword would be on the
outside. Of course, it was defensive as well, because it
meant you were harder to attack if you kept a potential
attacker to your left."

"Amazing," said Lisa.

"It seems that way, I know, but it wouldn't have seemed so amazing a hundred years ago. Back then, everybody had and used horses every day. They had as much to do with people's lives as cars influence the way we live now. Today almost every house has a garage, or at least nearby parking. Back then, almost every house had a stable, or at least a nearby livery stable."

It was utterly logical but something Lisa had not considered. Not so very long ago, horses interwove with almost every aspect of life, from farmwork to transportation to the development of roads and even customs of the road.

"Maybe I should be writing about more than military history," said Lisa.

"No, I think you'll find that there's plenty to write about on that one subject. Did you ever hear about Shakespeare's play *Richard the Third?*"

"Sure, but I never read it," said Lisa. She had always thought of herself as a good reader, but she had hardly begun Shakespeare.

"Well, King Richard's final words are 'A horse! A horse! My kingdom for a horse!' "

"I guess I'd better look that one up," said Lisa.

"It's a good story," Tiffani told her. "But historians have pretty much refuted the part about the little princes."

"What?"

"Well, you'll see, but that part doesn't have anything to do with horses."

Tiffani not only knew just about everything there was to know about horses, she also knew about literature and history. Lisa was totally impressed.

Carole returned then with a book that included a picture of the Mongolian wild horse, and since it was the perfect size, she simply made a copy of it and colored it with her colored pencils.

"Done!" she declared.

"Good work," Tiffani said. "And good timing, too, because I told my aunt she could pick me up right now." She stacked her books and all the charts, said good-bye to Carole and Lisa, and headed for the door.

"She's really something," said Carole.

"Definitely," Lisa agreed. "Wait'll I tell you all the stuff she was talking about when you were looking for that last picture. It'll blow Stevie away, too."

"Speaking of whom, what time were we supposed to be over at her house?"

"Whenever we get there," Lisa said.

Carole looked at her watch. "I guess that means about fifteen minutes from now, right?"

"Right."

It took them a few minutes to tidy up, packing away the scissors and glue and picking up the scraps of paper. It was a rule of the workroom that you left it as neat as you'd found it.

Five minutes later, they were headed for Stevie's house, both of them feeling very good about the work they'd gotten done. Carole's whole project was finished, a full week ahead of time. Lisa had just about all the information she needed to do her own project, and, true to the project's name, she was definitely learning something new.

Carole rang the bell and then stepped back. It didn't take long for the door to open, but when it did, Carole wasn't absolutely sure she was at the right house. She didn't really recognize the person standing in the doorway. She glanced around her quickly. The three bikes piled on the lawn and the slightly crushed but freshly weeded flower bed confirmed that it was, in fact, the Lakes'.

"Come on in, guys!"

The voice was right, too.

The door swung wide and Carole and Lisa walked in.

"Is Phil still here?" Lisa asked.

"No, his mom picked him up about an hour ago. After he left, I took a shower and changed my clothes," the person who resembled Stevie said.

"And everything else," said Lisa, staring at the girl. She was pretty sure it was Stevie, though if someone had told her right then that Stevie and Alex were actually triplets and the Lakes had been hiding the other sister for years, it wouldn't really have surprised her.

Stevie was wearing a pair of linen pants and a flowered blouse that matched the description Stevie had given her friends of "the awfulest Christmas present" she'd received last year. Not only was it flowered, but it had puffed sleeves with white lace trim.

The pants did not vaguely resemble any jeans Stevie had ever worn because (a) they didn't have any tears in them; and (b) nobody's phone number was scribbled on them in ballpoint pen. They were clean linen pants. And instead of sneakers, Stevie was wearing ballet flats, with bows. Moreover, her blouse and her pants appeared to have been ironed. Carole and Lisa had both had the opportunity to witness Mrs. Lake's frequent lectures to Stevie about looking after her clothes, which often included a reminder about where the iron was kept in the house. It wasn't a fact that had ever appeared to have sunk in. Except today. Stevie looked almost crisp.

"You okay?" Carole asked, genuinely concerned by the transformation in her friend.

"Sure, why would you ask that?"

"Well, the—"

"What about your *hair*?" Lisa asked, noticing for the first time that Stevie's normally straight dirty blond hair was now a mass of curls.

"I borrowed my mother's curling iron. Isn't it cool?"

"Yeah, your hair . . . ," Carole added, still absorbing the changes.

"It only took about half an hour once the hair was

dry," Stevie said. "I guess I'm going to have to get up a little earlier in the morning, but it's definitely worth it."

Up early? Stevie's usual idea of being up early was being out of bed five minutes before it was time to leave the house. She was often seen running down the street still combing her hair or pulling a sweater over her head.

"I guess I just sort of got tired of the way I was looking," Stevie said. "There's nothing wrong with a change every now and then, right?"

"Nothing wrong with a change," Lisa agreed. But this was more than a change. This was an entire taste transplant, and it didn't seem like Stevie.

The final touch was when Stevie invited her friends up to her room, one of their favorite places to gather. She opened the door to a spotlessly clean room, then turned to Lisa and Carole.

"Y'all come in now?"

9.

IT WASN'T THAT it hadn't been a fun time with her friends, Stevie thought, but sometimes it was just nice to be alone. Carole and Lisa had both had to leave very early that Sunday morning. Lisa, of course, had homework to do. She always had homework to do. Lisa could find homework to do even over summer vacation.

Carole was spending the morning with her father. That was one of the really nice things about Carole and her dad. Not only were they father and daughter, but they really liked being father and daughter and spending time together. That day, Carole had said, her father wanted to take her to a nearby Civil War battlefield. Carole had promised Lisa she'd bring her any material they had about horses in the battle.

74

Stevie had nothing to do. She had no homework—
or at least she only had homework she could more or
less ignore. Her parents were going antiquing and then
having lunch with a classmate of her father's from law
school. The Lake children had been invited to come
along, but none of them really liked this man. In fact,
Stevie wasn't convinced her father liked him much, either, but that was what they were doing with their Sunday.

It was only seven o'clock. Stevie's brothers were still
asleep. Stevie was essentially alone. She'd finished
breakfast and her friends had helped her clean up before they left. She was going riding, but not until late
morning. She had time for whatever she wanted.

It was high time she did some laundry. Mr. and Mrs.
Lake expected their children to wash their own clothes.
They could get help with tough stuff like ironing or
washing on the delicate cycle, but they were essentially
in charge. For Stevie that generally meant a monthly
project. When the stack of dirty clothes in her closet
became taller than she was, she'd bite the bullet and
get the job done.

She went back up to her room, made the bed, tidied
up the bathroom, folded the towels she and her friends
had used, and put them back on the rack. Then she
turned her attention to her closet.

When she opened the door, she was nearly bowled

over by dirty clothes tumbling out of the overstuffed space. She stood back and let the clothes fall where they would. Then she shook her head in dismay, disappointed in herself for letting the situation get so bad.

"Dirty clothes don't make a good impression," she said to herself, clucking her tongue.

It took a while to sort them all—whites, colors, delicates, and heavy-duty dirty. The last category was mostly jeans and barn clothes.

She hauled the first pile to the laundry room and began the tedious job of doing the wash. It wasn't that bad, really. The machines did all the work. She only had to sort, load, add the right chemicals, and wait.

She did delicates first because they'd dry the fastest, and then the permanent press stuff, followed by cottons and so on. When the first load was in, she brought the rest downstairs and lined them up on the floor next to the washing machine. They looked a little bit like schoolchildren standing in line in the cafeteria.

Schoolchildren reminded her that she actually did have some homework. She went upstairs to fetch her book bag, brought it back down, and set up a study center at the kitchen table.

First was prealgebra. Stevie didn't like to admit it, but she sort of liked prealgebra. The arithmetic wasn't very hard—nothing like, for instance, long division. And when she got the right answer, it was sort of tidy and satisfying. When she found that $X = 2$, she knew it was right. She wasn't so confident about $Y = 13.76598$. She did that problem again until it came out to $Y = 7$. That was right. She smiled, satisfied.

By the time the colors were in the dryer, Stevie really was finished with her homework. She'd read eight pages of history and answered six questions about plate tectonics. There was an English paper due at the end of the week, but she'd finished the reading and she'd have more time later to do an outline.

When the whites were dry, she switched loads, drying colors and washing heavy-duties.

She folded all the clothes that were dry so far and then picked a pretty white blouse out of the stack to wear. It looked clean, but it had some wrinkles. She located the iron and ironing board and pressed the blouse. It looked much better. She took it upstairs and laid it on her bed while she showered and washed her hair.

Her new hairdo did take longer, but the curls were so different from what she was accustomed to that they made her smile. Then she put on her pressed blouse, retrieved a clean pair of riding pants from the dryer, and pulled on a fresh pair of socks and her boots. She found her riding helmet and set it out to take with her, but a second glance told her it needed some work. It was covered with dust and straw. She found her mother's lint brush and took the helmet out onto the back porch to clean it. It only took a little while before the pretty black velvet emerged from the dust.

Back upstairs, she spotted herself in the mirror in her room and immediately recognized the need for some lip gloss and a hint of blush. She smiled back at the face in the mirror. She looked good, but she needed something else, just a little something. What was it?

Stevie began combing through her drawers. An accessory. Something with a little color to brighten her outfit. And there it was—a baby blue pullover sweater with decorative seed pearls outlining a kitten. So cute! She remembered that it had been a gift from some relative last year. Why hadn't she ever worn it before?

It was almost time to leave, but first Stevie finished folding her laundry and put it all away. Then she was out the door, headed for Pine Hollow.

Everybody was busy at the stable. The only one who actually greeted her was Belle. Max was teaching a class, and Red was busy with a colicky horse. Mrs. Reg was on the phone with someone who apparently was considering boarding his horse at Pine Hollow and wanted to know everything about the place, from the quality of the other horses there to the number of nails that had been used to put the stable together.

Stevie was essentially alone, and that suited her just fine.

She gave Belle a quick grooming and then went into

the tack room. She took her bridle off the hook but left her saddle there. She was ready to learn something new.

She found the two sidesaddles that belonged to the stable. One of them looked as if it would fit Belle better than the other, so she took that one with her back to Belle's stall.

Belle gave Stevie a very funny look when she saw the saddle, but she behaved as well as she always did while Stevie tacked her up. Looking at her own handiwork, Stevie shook her head. It seemed very strange indeed. But then that was probably because neither she nor Belle was used to it.

"Come on, girl," she said, clucking gently to the mare. "Let's go someplace where nobody can see us and try out this contraption."

Max had his class in the main schooling ring. That was what Stevie was hoping for, because it left the side paddock for her and Belle. She walked the horse out the side door, touching the good-luck horseshoe as she passed it. She had the feeling she was going to need it.

Maybe I'm being too pessimistic, she told herself. *I'm smart and capable. And, after all, in the last twenty-four hours, I've changed my hairstyle, washed all my clothes, ironed a blouse, cleaned my riding helmet, and finished my homework. Could anything be impossible?*

She drew Belle to a halt at the mounting block. Now came the first challenge. She thought about her method of attack. It wasn't like sitting in a chair, but it wasn't like climbing into a regular saddle, either. She'd seen Tiffani do it half a dozen times; she had even watched Lisa do it, but she had no idea how they'd managed.

"Nothing like simply trying," she said to herself and to Belle, who looked back at her curiously. Stevie put her left foot in the stirrup, hiked herself up and back at the same time, and ended up in the dirt on the far side of a rather confused Belle.

Stevie stood up, dusted herself off to regain her dignity, and returned to the mounting block. It took a few more tries, none of which she thought would appear in any sidesaddle riding manuals, and finally worked out a sort of compromise that involved swinging her right leg up over Belle's back end and then hiking it up over Belle's withers to get her knee into the hook on the left side of the saddle. If the style was questionable, the result was not. Stevie was in the saddle, not the dirt.

It took a few seconds for her to adjust her weight in a way that made any sense to her. Rather than sitting into the saddle, she was more resting on it. That was going to change everything, and that was what learning something new was all about.

She gently flicked the reins to the right, and Belle obediently turned in that direction, but there was no forward movement. *Hmmm.* How could she tell the mare to move ahead when she could only give her half a signal?

Normally the signal to walk came when a rider squeezed gently with her legs. Now all Stevie could do was squeeze Belle's left side, because that was the only place she had any legs in this saddle.

She put pressure on Belle's belly with her left leg. Belle moved to the right. That was perfectly logical. Horses had a natural inclination to move away from pressure, and they were trained to follow that inclination. Stevie tried again, and Belle did the same thing.

"Okay, girl," Stevie said gently but firmly. "We're playing with different rules today, okay? And the trouble is that neither of us knows what they are."

Stevie decided she should try to equalize the pressure by using her riding crop on the horse's right side. She didn't slap Belle or anything, but when she used her leg on one side, she pressed her crop against Belle's belly on the other. It might not have been what the proper sidesaddle rider would do, but Belle understood what she wanted. They moved forward.

"Whew," said Stevie.

And that was the way the whole hour went. Every time Stevie tried one signal, Belle misunderstood it until Stevie figured out a way to equalize her signals. Within the hour, she'd figured out how to get Belle to walk, trot, and turn. She even devised a sort of posting system at the trot that was almost easier than when riding astride because of the rest for her right leg. It was also more precarious because it was so hard to figure out how to balance.

Stevie was pretty sure Belle didn't like any of it one bit more than she did, but Belle was as willing as she was to give it a try. When she pulled the mare up to the final halt of the afternoon, Stevie leaned forward to give her a great big well-deserved hug, the result of which was that she totally lost her balance and slid right out of the saddle and onto the ground.

"I guess that means I don't have to figure out how to dismount, eh?" she asked Belle. Belle snorted. Stevie thought she knew what that meant.

Even though it had been hard, even though most of it seemed futile, Stevie felt good about the ride. She dusted herself off, took the reins, and walked Belle back to her stall. It wasn't often in riding that Stevie faced so many challenges in an hour. It wasn't as if she'd learned a lot about sidesaddle riding, but she'd learned a lot about figuring things out, and that was always satisfying for her.

Belle seemed to sigh with relief when the sidesaddle came off. Stevie took it back to the tack room and then returned to give her horse a quick grooming and some fresh water. When she was returning to Belle's stall for a final good-bye, she passed the little mirror over the sink in the tack room and saw herself for the first time in a couple of hours. She was startled. It was almost as if it weren't Stevie who looked back at her.

The girl she saw wasn't wearing a soiled T-shirt. She was wearing an ironed white blouse. She wasn't wearing a torn sweatshirt. She was wearing a pale blue sweater with seed pearls. Sure, it had gotten a few smudges of dirt from the two tumbles she had taken, but it was still pale blue and pretty. The girl in the mirror didn't have straight dirty blond hair. She had curls—a lot of them. She was Stevie, all right—the new and improved Stevie. She paused for a moment, smiling at the girl, who smiled back. She could almost imagine someone standing behind her—one Phil Marsten, smiling broadly, warmly, and lovingly. "Elegant, feminine, and charming," Phil's image seemed to say, squeezing her shoulders gently.

Filled with a new and improved confidence, Stevie bade Belle farewell and headed for home.

10

WHEN STEVIE GOT HOME, her parents had returned from their visit with Mr. Lake's friend. Stevie greeted them quickly and retreated upstairs. She barely registered her mother's furrowed brow as she passed by.

Once out of the shower, Stevie slipped into a clean pair of jeans and a clean, carefully folded T-shirt, but as soon as she saw herself in the mirror, she changed her mind. That wouldn't do at all. Neither would the droopy straight hair. She dried her hair, fluffing it with her fingers as best she could because she didn't want to borrow her mother's curling iron when her mother was at home. The finished product looked pretty good. Then it was time to choose her wardrobe for the rest of the day.

It took a while. In fact, it took a long time. Stevie hadn't realized how totally devoid of suitable clothes her wardrobe was. Her mother was right. She needed some new clothes and she needed them right away. Finally she settled on her only non-denim pair of slacks, some yellow ones that were a little too big. She found a blouse that more or less went with them and a knit top. It wasn't as nice as the blue sweater with seed pearls, but it would do.

She pulled on some socks and school shoes, since she didn't want to wear sneakers, and went downstairs.

Her mother did a slight double take when she saw Stevie, but she said nothing. Stevie noticed it and took that as a compliment on her new fashion sense.

"Mom, you're right about something."

"Where's the band and fireworks?" Mrs. Lake teased.

"Well, even a swell mom like you will be right about something every once in a while," Stevie responded, going along with the joke.

"And it is . . . ?"

"I need some new clothes."

"Oh, I don't know, sweetheart. Some of those jeans of yours, with the seven or eight tears on each leg—well, they're just barely getting broken in. You should be able to get two or three more years of wear out of them."

Stevie smiled, recognizing her own words. But that

had been before—long before—when she hadn't realized what some good taste and a fresh look at her style could do for her.

"Well, but I was wondering if we could go shopping this afternoon?"

"You mean, like now?" Mrs. Lake asked, looking at the newspaper she was clearly intending to read.

"If that's okay with you," Stevie said.

"I will not miss an opportunity to take you shopping when you're actually willing," said Mrs. Lake. She stood up, grabbed the magazine section with the crossword puzzle in it, picked up her car keys and pocketbook, reached for a jacket, and said, "We're off."

Stevie followed her out the door.

The mall was a twenty-minute drive from their house. While they drove, Stevie tried to give her mother an idea of what she thought she needed: a couple of pairs of slacks, perhaps a skirt or two, some blouses that didn't look like little-girl things or as if they were just for dress-up.

"But they might need to be ironed," said Mrs. Lake.

"That's okay," Stevie said. "I don't mind."

Mrs. Lake drove back into the lane she'd been driving in before Stevie had stunned her.

"And I want some sweaters, too," said Stevie.

"You've got drawers full of sweatshirts," said Mrs. Lake.

"No, I mean like sweaters that go with the skirts and

86

the blouses, not just to keep warm, but, you know, *pretty* sweaters."

"You mean, you want, like, *clothes*," said Mrs. Lake.

"Right, that's what I mean," said Stevie.

"Wow," said Mrs. Lake, pulling into a parking place by the mall's main department store.

When they walked into the store, the first person they saw was Veronica diAngelo. Veronica rarely missed an opportunity to shop, but she usually did so at the more exclusive shops.

"Oh, what are you doing here?" Veronica asked rather disdainfully.

Before Stevie answered, the thought flashed through her head that Veronica was capable of asking the time of day disdainfully. Disdain was her principal attitude.

"I'm looking for some new clothes," Stevie answered. And then, in a moment of weakness inspired by the fact that Veronica was always impeccably dressed, she asked: "Any suggestions where I should shop?"

"The Salvation Army Thrift Shop is on the other end of the mall, as you no doubt remember," said Veronica.

Stevie opened her mouth to make a withering retort, but she stopped herself. Hassling with Veronica was definitely not elegant, feminine, or charming.

"Come on, Mom," she said instead. "Let's see what they have in the juniors' department here." The two of them headed for the escalator.

"What an ill-behaved child that Veronica is," said Mrs. Lake. "She always reminds me of her mother."

"Way to go, Mom!" Stevie agreed.

In the sweater area Stevie and her mother ran into Carole and Lisa.

"Hey!" Carole greeted her.

"Stevie's shopping!" said Lisa.

"Well, I need some new clothes, but what are you two doing here?" Stevie asked. Happy as she was to see her friends, a small part of her had hoped to sort of surprise them with her new look. That was okay, though. They could be part of the change, and that would be just as much fun.

"When Dad and I finished touring the battlefield, I had so much information for Lisa on horses in the battle that I called her, and it turned out the best place for us to meet was right here. Nothing wrong with that, is there?"

"Nothing at all," said Stevie.

"Um," Mrs. Lake interrupted. The girls all looked at her. "If you three want to spend time together, I could go get myself a cup of coffee at the food court. And then you could come get me when you need me and my credit card."

"Oh, sure," said Lisa. "Shopping with Stevie's easy: four pairs of jeans and six T-shirts and we're done. We know where to find you."

"Don't forget the sweats," said Carole.

"We'll be fine," said Stevie. Her mother waved good-bye to the girls and pulled the crossword puzzle out of her handbag.

"Okay, jeans first," said Lisa.

"Nope," Stevie said. "I've got all the jeans I need. T-shirts and sweats, too. No, what I need is some real clothes—like this," she said, indicating her outfit.

"I thought you hated those pants because they're too big for you," Carole said.

"I thought you hated them because they're ugly," Lisa added.

"Well, I do hate them, but I want ones that are a decent fit and a nice color. I want clothes that are real clothes. It's not a rule that I have to look like a slob *all* the time."

"I've gotten so used to the slob look—" Carole began.

"Not *all* the time," Lisa said sharply.

Carole changed directions. "Okay, well, we can find something that isn't grungy that'll be good for you. Why don't we go over to Simpson's?"

Simpson's was a store that catered to juniors. It had a wide variety of clothes, and both Lisa and Carole liked the selection. Neither of them had ever thought it would interest Stevie, but perhaps today was an exception.

Stevie considered her friends' general taste in clothes. She'd always known that the three of them had personal styles as different as their personalities. Lisa always wore clothes that were extremely conservative but still fashionable. Most people would describe them as preppy. Carole's clothes were simple, never fussy, and always neat and clean. That was surely inherited from her father's Marine Corps sense of style. Stevie, on the other hand, tended to assemble outfits from among whatever was the cleanest in her closet, and sometimes the results were very interesting—hardly ever stylish, but definitely interesting. Now she was determined to make a change.

When the three of them entered Simpson's, Lisa was immediately drawn to the rack of skirts and slacks, while Carole headed for the nearby stacks of button-downs. Stevie disappeared to look at the cotton sweaters.

"What do you think she wants?" Carole asked Lisa.

"Nice stuff, I guess. Look, here are some nice navy blue slacks. They're permanent press, so they won't wrinkle. But navy shows spills. Maybe something like gray would be better." Lisa took a couple of pairs off the rack for Stevie to try on. Then she found some nice pleated skirts in soft plaids that might do for Stevie. She took those, too.

"And look at these turtlenecks," said Carole. "This would go with the slacks, and this one with the skirts. Turtlenecks are great because you don't have to iron them and they always look neat. Black goes with everything. And this is a nice bright red. That's a good color for Stevie. You've got to have a white. And this hunter green is sharp-looking."

"Great stuff," said Lisa. "Now let's find Stevie."

Laden with clothes, the two tracked down their friend. It took a while because Stevie had apparently found a dressing room at the far end of the store. It only took a little convincing before the salesperson let Carole and Lisa into the room with Stevie.

When Stevie opened the door for them, she had already put on her first outfit. She was wearing pale yellow wool slacks, a white blouse with a frilly collar, and a matching pale yellow angora sweater.

"Isn't Phil just going to love this?" she asked.

Carole and Lisa were stunned. This was so unlike Stevie that it overwhelmed them, even more than the curly hair and the strange outfit had the day before.

Before she could stop herself, Lisa asked, "Phil who?"

"Marsten," Stevie said, surprised that Lisa had to ask. "Is there another Phil who cares what I wear?"

"I'm sorry," Lisa said. "I never thought Phil particularly noticed what you wore—I mean, not that he doesn't care when you dress up for something, but most of the time the two of you are at a stable and—"

"*Angora?*" Carole interrupted

"It's so *soft!*" Stevie said. "Here, feel it." Carole obliged. It was soft. It just wasn't Stevie. "And look at all these other wonderful clothes I found. I haven't tried them all on yet, but I know I'm going to love them! Coming to Simpson's was a great idea!"

She pointed to the stack of slacks, skirts, blouses, and sweaters she'd found for herself. All pastel. There were three other angora sweaters—"Though of course I can't buy them all," Stevie confided. "But I know Phil will love everything. It's just so wonderful to find exactly what I was looking for. Now, stand by while I try it all on and help me decide what I've got to have and what I can't take, okay?"

Stunned to silence, Carole and Lisa sat down on the little seats in the dressing room and watched while Stevie put on and critiqued outfit after outfit. Lace, chenille, wool, crisp cotton. Iron, iron, dry clean, iron. Nothing wash-and-wear, and nothing that could ever be worn more than once before cleaning.

There was nothing wrong with any of the clothes. They were of good quality, and Stevie had found outfits that went together very nicely. They just didn't go with Stevie—or at least with the Stevie her friends thought they knew.

As Stevie closed in on her choices, she sent Carole and Lisa out in search of her mother and her mother's credit card.

"We'd better give her some warning," Lisa said as they approached.

"About how Stevie's body has been taken over by a pastel-loving alien?" Carole asked.

"We might try to find a nicer way to put it," Lisa suggested.

Mrs. Lake looked up when the girls arrived at the table. "Is she done already?" she asked.

"Almost," Carole said. "But I think she may surprise you a little bit."

"She already has," said Mrs. Lake. "I've never known her to actually *want* to buy anything other than jeans. I've sort of prepared myself that this is going to be a more expensive shopping trip than most."

"Well, there's that," said Lisa. "And then . . ."

"Yes?"

"Well, there's what she's chosen," said Carole. "It's not her usual."

"What good news," said Mrs. Lake. "Isn't it about time Stevie actually took some interest in clothes?"

"Right," agreed Lisa. She and Carole simultaneously thought it was best to let Stevie speak for herself, and then if Mrs. Lake wanted to make any reports about UFO's . . .

MONDAY, STEVIE HAD A ten-minute break between pre-
algebra and French, just long enough to duck into the
girls' room to make sure her curls were in place and to
touch up her lipstick—two things she couldn't remember ever doing on her class break before. She had
started to open the girls' room door when she heard her
name spoken inside.

"Can you believe that getup Stevie's wearing today?"
It was Meg Durham, one of Veronica's friends, so it was
no surprise whose voice answered.

"And the hairdo," said Veronica. The two of them
dissolved into giggles.

"Jealousy," Stevie said to herself, letting the door
close. There was another girls' room at the other end of
the hall. It was empty when she got there, giving her

some privacy in which to admire her own reflection while fluffing her curls and replacing the lipstick.

She'd never really thought yellow was her color, but this pale shade seemed to do something for her. It was very ladylike and elegant. Stevie smiled back at herself, brushed some imaginary lint from her shoulder, and returned to the hallway. She was all ready for French. She could take anything today, partly because she liked her new clothes so much and partly because after school she was going to Pine Hollow. Time for sidesaddle lesson number two.

AT THE STABLE, Stevie had to ask Mrs. Reg if she could hang her slacks and sweater in the office rather than in her locker. The locker room was so full of dust that she was sure the clothes would get soiled.

"Whatever you want, Stevie," Mrs. Reg said, regarding her curiously.

"Thanks," Stevie answered, pleased by the compliment she was pretty sure Mrs. Reg had just given her.

She stopped by the tack room on her way to Belle's stall and picked up the sidesaddle and Belle's bridle. Belle welcomed her with almost the same strange look she'd been getting from everybody all day long. In this case, she knew it was because Belle recognized the saddle.

"Don't worry, girl," she promised the horse. "I

learned a thing or two the last time, and I promise it'll go better today."

Belle stood still while Stevie tacked her up. She walked patiently toward the ring, pausing, with Stevie, at the good-luck horseshoe. Stevie managed to mount Belle on the first try. She shifted her weight about on her bottom and her thigh until she was pretty sure she was balanced.

She clucked her tongue and flicked the reins, giving Belle a little nudge with her left heel at the same time.

For Belle, that was a lot of signals at once. She took off at a trot. Stevie reined her in a little. The mare halted. Stevie signaled her to start again just using her leg, and this time Belle moved to the right.

"Oh dear," said Stevie.

After such a rotten beginning to the lesson, there was nowhere to go but up. Experience had taught Stevie that sometimes when a ride began really badly—and this one had all the earmarks of that—the best thing to do was to start again.

Reluctantly she slid out of the saddle, walked Belle back to the mounting block, and climbed back onto the horse.

Belle stood quietly, waiting for instructions.

"Walk," said Stevie, putting some ever-so-gentle pressure on her left side with her leg and on her right side with the riding crop. Miraculously, Belle walked.

Stevie was annoyed with herself for forgetting about the riding crop in the first place.

The rest of the hour was just about as successful as the first ten minutes had been. Right turns were easy. Left turns were hard. Gait changes were a nightmare when Stevie forgot to use the crop and merely ragged when she remembered. She hadn't felt so much like a rank beginner since the day she'd been one. And none of it was Belle's fault. The two of them were learning together—willing pupils, but pupils nonetheless.

Both pupils were nearly exhausted by the time Stevie led Belle back into the stable and gave her a well-deserved grooming. She was halfway home before she remembered she was still wearing her riding clothes and had left her lovely new yellow outfit in Mrs. Reg's closet.

If it hadn't been her favorite of all her new outfits, she might have just left it there. But it was her favorite, and Pine Hollow was no place for good clothes. Exhausted but determined, she returned and carried the pale yellow outfit back home.

The good news that helped her all the way home was the knowledge that she had a riding class on Wednesday, when she and Belle would ride the usual way, the normal way, the right way—astride. She sighed in anticipation.

*   *   *

ON WEDNESDAY, she asked Mrs. Reg if she could leave her angora sweater in her office.

"Don't worry," said Mrs. Reg, looking at the sweater with a furrowed brow. "It'll be safe here. Nobody will steal it, that's for sure."

Stevie wondered briefly why Mrs. Reg was so sure about that, but that wasn't why she was leaving it with her. It was that the locker room was totally dusty and would mess up that pretty, pure white.

"Thanks," said Stevie.

When Stevie and Belle reached the schooling ring, she found that Lisa and Tiffani were already there. They'd apparently arranged to meet before class so that Tiffani could give Lisa some help with her sidesaddle riding.

Some of the other students were there, too, watching. Carole and Starlight were over to one side. Stevie joined them.

"Okay, now, Lisa, I don't think that was what you wanted to do at all? That little ole Diamond is just waiting for a signal from you? He's gonna do anything you tell him? So why don't you go ahead and tell him to go to the left?"

Lisa used her left hand to open the rein on the left side, maintaining a true balance in the saddle. Diamond paused a short moment and then turned to the left.

"Great!" said Tiffani. "That was just about perfect?"

"That wasn't perfect," Stevie whispered to Carole.

"Of course it wasn't," said Carole. "Lisa knows that and so does everybody else here. Lisa should have been able to give a signal that didn't confuse Diamond for that little second that he paused before doing what he was told. On the other hand, it was definitely better than her earlier try. And look, Lisa's smiling, not because she's done something really good, but because she's done something better. That's what learning is," Carole told Stevie.

Stevie looked around. Everybody was watching Lisa's lesson, and it couldn't have been easy for her or even for Tiffani. The two of them proceeded, working on improving Lisa's turning techniques. It occurred to Stevie that perhaps she could learn a thing or two about sidesaddle riding by listening carefully, but she found her mind wandering—to Tiffani's clothes.

As usual, Tiffani was wearing pastels. This time her jodhpurs were baby blue instead of the pink of the previous week. She was wearing a pink blouse with a baby blue sweater over it. Stevie didn't like that sweater as much as her own with the seed pearls, but it was a nice style. On the other hand . . .

"Look!" Stevie whispered to Carole, unable to contain herself.

"What?" Carole said.

"That blue sweater—"

"Not very practical in a riding ring, that's for sure," said Carole.

"It doesn't match her eyes at all. She'd need a blue with much more gray in it than that—and paler, too."

Before Carole could respond, Stevie turned her attention back to something going on in the ring.

Carole picked up her dropped jaw without saying anything, because there was almost no way to respond when Stevie Lake, her very best friend in the world, seemed to have sustained a personality change. First her strange shopping spree and then worrying about Tiffani's shade of pale blue? Carole made a note to herself to talk with Lisa after class. Something seemed to be terribly wrong with Stevie, and perhaps her mother hadn't noticed. The two girls might consider convincing her to take Stevie to a doctor, preferably one who might examine her head.

Carole was relieved when Max came into the ring and called the class to order. Perhaps a return to routine would help set Stevie's mind straight.

Class was great, as usual, and Carole was pleased to see that Stevie was almost completely normal through it, if one didn't count the fact that she actually raised her hand every time she wanted to speak and that she never interrupted anyone or made any smart remarks, even missing a golden opportunity when Veronica got turned around and rode in the opposite direction from everyone else in the class.

As soon as Veronica did that, the other students glanced at Stevie, waiting for a smart remark. But none came.

At the end of the class, Max reminded the riders, almost all of whom were also in Horse Wise, that they were supposed to be working on their Learn Something New project, and he was willing to help anybody or to pair anyone with a classmate for help if they needed it.

A few of the students had questions, and Max set aside time to answer them after class. Then he looked at Stevie.

"And you, Ms. Lake? Do you need any help with your project—um, whatever it is?"

It was a leading question, but Stevie didn't follow. If Carole's eyes didn't deceive her, Stevie actually blushed, a most un-Stevian mannerism.

"No, Max, I don't need any help," Stevie said.

Carole sighed with relief. When Stevie acted like that, it was a sure sign that she didn't have a project started yet, and the fact that the project was supposed to be finished in three days was only just beginning to bother her. Now, *that* was Stevie, pure Stevie. It was possible that an alien had taken over a good portion of her mind and body, but the conversion wasn't total. There was still some of the old, beloved Stevie there, and that meant there was still hope.

STEVIE HUMMED ALL the way home from her riding class, barely aware of the confused looks she'd gotten from her classmates on her way out of the stable as she carried her white angora sweater. That night was going to be a very special night. She and Phil had a study date.

Sometimes it happened on a Wednesday night that Mrs. Marsten had a committee meeting in Willow Creek. She was willing to bring Phil and drop him off at Stevie's while she went to her meeting, as long as the two of them promised to get some work done. They usually found a way to finish an algebra problem or two, or maybe they'd talk a little bit about history, but it was mostly just fun to get together.

Stevie had all sorts of plans for that night. For one

thing, she was pretty sure she had time to do some baking for Phil. She wanted to make his favorite cookies, chocolate chip. In the past, Stevie had taken a fair amount of grief from her friends about her cooking, and even she would admit that it wasn't her greatest skill. In fact, she teased herself, it was even possible that she was better at sidesaddle riding than she was at cooking, but what could be so hard about baking chocolate chip cookies?

The kitchen was empty when she got there. As quickly as she could, she assembled all the ingredients listed on the back of the bag of chocolate morsels. Well, they didn't actually have all of the ingredients, but they had most of them. She couldn't find any walnuts, but she decided peanuts would do instead.

It didn't take long to make the cookies—less than an hour for the whole batch. As soon as they were out of the oven, she put them on a plate, covered them with plastic wrap, and left them on the counter. She plastered the wrap with notes, threatening death and worse if any of her brothers ate so much as one crumb.

Then she hurried upstairs to shower and wash her hair. Time was getting short, and she wanted to be all ready—in one of her new outfits—when Phil arrived.

She was only halfway through the curling process when Phil got there. This wasn't good news, because if Phil should happen to spend any time alone with any of her brothers while waiting for her, her brothers were likely to say things Stevie wouldn't want said to her boyfriend. She called downstairs to him.

Alex answered instead of Phil. "Don't worry, Stevie. We'll take care of him while you try to cover up some of those warts that have been popping up on your nose. Also, did you find the lice shampoo where Mom left it for you?"

Just what Stevie was afraid of.

"I'll be down in a minute, Phil, but don't you pay any attention to anything my silly brothers say, now, will you?"

"I promise not to," Phil called back up the stairs. "As long as Alex lets me beat him at Nok Hockey."

Stevie heard the two boys thunder down to the basement. She was philosophical. There wasn't anything she could do except finish curling her hair, and she was sure that when Phil saw the final results, he'd be so bowled over that he wouldn't even remember any of the awful things Alex might say.

Ten minutes later, Stevie walked into the rec room. Phil and Alex were playing an intense game, calling fouls and shouting at one another happily.

Nobody saw her enter.

"Yoo-hoo," she said.

"Uh, hi," said Phil, glancing up quickly, then returning his attention to the game.

"Uh—*huh?*" Phil looked back up, shooting the

wooden puck at a wall some fifteen feet beyond the goal on the board. "Stevie?" he asked.

Stevie smiled. *It's probably the curls*, she thought. Phil had never seen her with anything but straight hair, usually just hanging down. And now there she was, transformed into a lovely, feminine, and elegant creature.

"Angora?" Phil said, confused.

"Want to pat it?" Stevie invited.

Alex pointed his finger into his throat as if to make himself vomit, but Phil didn't notice. He couldn't take his eyes off Stevie. She beamed with pleasure at his gaze.

"Uh, no, um, thanks," Phil said, embarrassed.

Stevie was a little disappointed. Not that she expected him to take her up on the invitation, but she'd sort of hoped he'd be a little more flirtatious, just the way he'd been with Tiffani. *Well*, she told herself, *he just isn't used to the new, transformed me. Give him a minute. Maybe five.*

Just then Mrs. Lake called the family to dinner. Alex and Phil put the Nok Hockey away, arguing about the final score of their match as they did so.

Stevie got out of their way by going upstairs to help her mother put the food on the table. It wasn't her night to do that, it was Chad's, but there were no rules saying a girl couldn't be kind and helpful when she wanted to be.

"Oh, that's one of your new outfits," her mother said. "I never would have thought of you in snowy angora." She handed Stevie a platter of chicken.

At least Mom knows how to react to a nice outfit, thought Stevie.

When they were seated at the table, Stevie was pleased to find all eyes on her. It even made her a little nervous.

"Pa*pa*," she asked, putting the emphasis on the second syllable, "would you like some chicken?"

" 'Pa*pa*'?" Chad echoed. "Who's that?"

"I think she means your father," Mrs. Lake suggested.

"I know that. I was just wondering who it was who was speaking," Chad said.

"Stevie," said Mrs. Lake. "That's your sister. I think you've met her before."

"Is this a costume party?" Michael asked, staring at Stevie. "Because if it is, can I put on my pirate costume?"

"Just eat your dinner," said Mrs. Lake.

"Mom, I didn't think we were allowed to bring pets to the table," said Alex. "Especially fluffy white kittens?"

Everybody turned to Stevie once again, waiting for her retort. Normally Stevie would have said something about guard dogs or farm animals being allowed at the table, or she would have answered with something more direct, like a blob of mashed potatoes.

"Why, Alex, you surely don't confuse me with a kitten?" she said instead. "It's just this soft fluffy sweater. Inside is your usual sweet, loving twin sister. I guess if I'm a kitten, then you're just a huggable teddy bear."

Chad choked. Phil stared. Even Mr. Lake couldn't help gaping.

Stevie smiled, pleased with herself. She'd managed to deflect an impending food fight with her newfound sweetness. It was a little bit like the way a certain member of her class that day had helped Lisa learn a new technique by being nice and encouraging instead of loading on the criticism.

"Phil, could I have some of those delicious peas?" Stevie asked, reaching for the bowl. As if in a trance, Phil picked up the bowl of peas and passed them over to the girl who was sitting across the table from him.

Most of the rest of the meal was consumed in silence. When Mrs. Lake asked the boys to clear the table, everybody stood up to clear at once. The dishes were stacked in the sink in a matter of minutes. Since Stevie had company, she was excused from putting them in the dishwasher. Grateful, she picked up the platter of chocolate chip cookies and winked at Phil. He picked up his history textbook and followed her down to the rec room.

The two of them settled onto the old sofa where they usually sat and worked and sometimes played. Stevie slipped off her shoes and tucked her legs under her comfortably while she uncovered the cookies.

"Aren't my brothers just a stitch?" she asked, smiling and blinking flirtatiously at Phil.

"Uh, sure," he answered. "Very funny."

It wasn't what Stevie had expected. She'd thought he'd say something funny in return about how it was nice to have somebody normal in the family—the kind of remark he often made to her.

"And Papa?"

Phil didn't actually answer that question. He did, however, reach over to Stevie, almost as she'd been hoping he would. But he wasn't reaching for a hug. He brushed his hand across her forehead affectionately.

No, that wasn't the word. It wasn't affectionate, though she wanted it to be. It was more businesslike than that. He'd paused halfway across her forehead, the same way her mother did when she was doing a quick temperature check. Did Phil think she was sick?

"Why, Phil, I'm just fine?" she told him.

"What?"

"I'm just fine?" she repeated.

"Is that a question?"

"No, silly boy. I'm telling you I'm fine. You don't have to check me for a temperature?"

"I don't?"

Why does he keep asking me questions? Stevie wondered. *What's going on here?*

Oh, of course! It was the cookies. There she was, sitting next to him on the sofa and holding an entire plateful of cookies, and she hadn't even offered him a nibble of one.

"I bet I know what you'd like," she said temptingly.

"You do?" he asked, almost a little nervous.

"You want one of these little ole cookies, don't you?"

"Uh—"

"Chocolate chips. Your favorite, right?"

"Right," Phil said. "I do love chocolate chips. Did you bake them yourself?"

"All by myself," she assured him.

"Oh," said Phil.

Stevie unwrapped the platter, being extra careful not to spill any crumbs on her sweater or slacks.

Phil studied the platter of cookies, and Stevie was pretty sure that he was simply picking the biggest, tastiest cookie for himself. She waited patiently, smiling all the while.

He made his selection, but when he attempted to pick it up, it was attached to all the other cookies around it. He tried for another. Same thing.

"Maybe you should have let them cool before you stacked them," he suggested.

"I forgot that part," Stevie said, a little embarrassed

that her new, improved self couldn't remember something that simple.

Eventually Phil managed to break off a chunk of the cookie loaf. He took a bite.

Stevie waited for the approval. It wasn't exactly forthcoming. The look on Phil's face was one of concern, and that quickly turned into something else altogether.

He gagged. "Did you follow the recipe?" he asked when he managed to get the bite down.

"Exactly," Stevie said. "Is something wrong?"

"Well, they're a little salty."

"The recipe does call for salt," said Stevie.

"But, like half a teaspoon or something, right?" Phil asked.

"Is *that* what that said?" Stevie asked, realizing that she'd misread the recipe and put in, instead, half a cup of salt. *Half a cup!* How could she do that? On this, a special night for her and Phil, one that she so wanted to go perfectly, she'd managed to make absolutely everything go wrong. She'd kept him waiting, made him play a game with her brother, forced him to eat dinner with her family. And he hadn't even noticed her pretty outfit, hadn't said anything in the slightest bit flirty, hadn't smiled, hadn't even held her hand, and now, to make it worse, she'd practically poisoned him!

She couldn't help it. No matter how hard she tried to hold it back, a tear escaped from her eye and began rolling down her cheek. She swept it away as quickly as she could, but it was only replaced by another and another.

Stevie reached for a tissue, but of course there weren't any in the rec room. Phil usually carried a handkerchief, one of his endearing qualities. She looked at him to provide it, but he was preoccupied. His shoulders were shaking in a familiar manner. His eyes were cast down at his lap, surely to avoid meeting hers. Then Stevie realized what was going on. He was laughing—in his own very Phil Marsten way.

"Are you laughing at my cooking?" she demanded, now a little angry.

Phil shook his head. "No, not at all," he said.

"Then exactly what is amusing you so?"

"It's relief," he said, pointing to the plate of cookies. "I'm laughing from relief."

"What are you talking about?" Stevie asked, truly confused by his bizarre behavior.

"It really *is* Stevie in there," he said, looking at her now.

"Of course it's Stevie," she said.

"Well, you could have fooled me," he said. "Until you got to baking. There are some things you can't hide."

"What are you talking about?" Stevie asked.

Before he could answer, Alex came clumping down the cellar steps. "Phil, your ma*ma*'s here," he said.

"And she's in a hurry. My mama said not to come back upstairs without you."

Phil stood up then and, saying good night to Stevie, carried the plate of cookies over to the stairs.

"Here you go, sport," he said to Alex. "I think Stevie would like you to have these. Good night, Stevie. If it's okay with you, I'm coming to Horse Wise on Saturday, and I'll see you then. And maybe afterward we can have a Saddle Club trail ride—you, me, Carole, and Lisa. Okay?"

"Sure," Stevie said, though at that moment she was completely unsure about everything, and nothing seemed okay.

She heard Phil reach the first floor and was aware of his speedy exit, but as he left, she wondered exactly who had left and what had gone on while he'd been there.

This was Phil, her longtime boyfriend. They knew one another very well. At least she thought they did. Stevie had anticipated every single reaction that her dear Phil was going to have to her new look and her new self, and she'd been wrong every time. The only thing she'd done that seemed to please him was nearly poison him with salt.

What in the world was going on?

112

IT WASN'T USUAL for Phil to come to Horse Wise. He belonged to Cross County, the Pony Club in his own town, and, like Horse Wise, they had their meetings on Saturday mornings. The fact that he was coming to Horse Wise meant he was missing Cross County— twice in two weeks. Stevie wondered why he was doing that.

Everything seemed normal at first. He greeted Stevie with his usual smile, informed her that he was still alive after the cookie fiasco (Stevie cringed a little, but he still didn't seem at all upset about her total failure in the kitchen), and settled down on the floor of Max's office next to her. Stevie was wearing clean jodhpurs, neatly polished boots, and a pink sweater. She had also curled her hair that morning, even though it meant getting up a half hour earlier than she was used to. Phil didn't say anything about the way she looked. Stevie wondered if she ought to get to the drugstore to buy some new makeup or perfume. She'd read about something called Magnolia Nights that sounded very alluring.

"Horse Wise, come to order!" Max called out in his usual manner. The room was quickly quiet. He welcomed everybody, especially Phil, and then made the usual bunch of announcements about horse events in the near future, impending competitions, and the next round of tests that would be administered for Pony Club ratings. When he was done with his announcements, he turned the floor over to Carole and Tiffani.

Carole opened up an easel, and Tiffani loaded a bunch of charts onto it.

"Horses have been around for a very long time," Carole began. "They are found on all the continents—except Antarctica."

"As soon as humans began domesticating horses, they found that some were better at certain kinds of tasks than others," Tiffani said. "That was when they began breeding horses to improve the skills that were important to them, and before too long they had helped nature create separate breeds. Some breeds are known for their strength, some for their speed, some for their gentle personalities, and some for endurance.

These are skills developed in nature but refined by humans. In the next few minutes, we will examine just a few of the breeds that can be found all around the world today. Carole?"

"Thank you, Tiffani," Carole said. She turned over the first chart.

Carole and Tiffani had broken down the breeds into geographical lines and then into groups. They'd done an enormous amount of work, showing the important bloodlines in each of the breeds. Tiffani spent a particularly long time explaining about the Tennessee walker, but Carole also had an opportunity to talk about Thoroughbreds—Starlight was half Thoroughbred.

Stevie and a lot of the other Horse Wise members actually knew much of what Carole and Tiffani were saying. Everybody knew that Friesians—the big black workhorses of Europe—were used to pull hearses. A lot of it was totally new, certainly to Stevie, who'd never heard of some of the Asian breeds that Carole talked about. Stevie knew that Carole had started out knowing a lot, but it was amazing to think what she must have had to study to learn all that she'd put into the report.

Nobody talked or interrupted throughout the whole presentation because it was so interesting and informative. Max sat at his desk, clearly as interested in what his students were saying as everybody else was.

When they were done, the whole room exploded in

applause. Stevie clapped, and so did Lisa, but Phil was doing more than that. He was practically whooping, obviously very glad that he'd come to Horse Wise instead of Cross County that morning. Stevie looked at him out of the corner of her eye, clapping away. Then she looked at Carole and Tiffani, both pleased with the response their audience was giving them and bowing occasionally.

Stevie leaned over to Phil and whispered, "I think Carole did most of the work on this. She knows almost all this stuff off the top of her head, you know?"

Phil looked at Stevie quizzically, but he didn't say anything. He just kept on clapping.

Max then announced the end of Horse Wise, but he told everybody to stay where they were.

"I know a lot of you have been working on your Learn Something New reports. If any of them begin to measure up to the great report we've just had from Carole and Tiffani, then we're all going to be learning a lot of new things today. I thought it would be best if we got our sandwiches and began right here in my office so that those of you who want to make presentations can. Then we'll go tack up and see what the rest of you have learned."

Everybody had something to contribute. Lisa was one of the first, giving her report on military riding and its influence on modern riding styles. April had decided to learn about different kinds of tack. She had made charts of English and Western tack and also worldwide variations—like the differences between American and Argentinean cowboy tack, as well as Arabian saddles and bridles.

Adam Levine had prepared a report on horse communication, complete with recordings of different neighing and whinnying sounds, as well as photographs showing variations of body language.

Meg Durham presented a report on braiding styles. Joe gave his report on the Bureau of Land Management. Betsy Cavanaugh read a whole paper on Olympic competitors. Olivia presented a book report on *Black Beauty*.

When the last presenter was done, the meeting finally broke up and moved to the schooling ring for the riding demonstrations.

There were all sorts of demonstrations. One rider showed how she'd learned to polish her pony's hooves. Another demonstrated how she made patterns on her pony's flank when she groomed him. It was a horse show trick, and it was a neat one. May Grover showed that she'd trained her pony, Macaroni, to respond to visual signals—to come when called, sometimes; to change gaits in the field; and to come over for a treat. That last signal was one he never failed to respond to. Veronica diAngelo, having abandoned her report on polo because it required too much work, showed how she'd learned to make her horse stand in absolutely proper form for conformation classes at horse shows.

"Not much of a trick there," Stevie whispered to Phil. He nodded. They both knew that Veronica's horse had been trained to do that long before she ever bought him. Nevertheless, the class applauded politely.

Two students had worked on driving. Corey had her pony, Samurai, hitched to the pony cart. He trotted around the ring a couple of times, and Corey showed how he could change gaits and directions. She'd done a good job and deserved the applause she got.

Josh had studied driving, too, but he was using the small carriage. He did just fine, but his pony was in a fussy mood. A fussy pony and a carriage made a bad combination, and Max told Josh to drive him out of the ring, promising to let him show what he'd learned on a day when his pony was in a better mood. People clapped anyway.

Then, when Tiffani brought out Diamond with his sidesaddle on, the six students she'd been working with all had their turns going around the ring sidesaddle. None of them was very good, but they all stayed on, and Diamond responded to their aids just right.

There was more applause.

"Well done, class," Max said. "So well done, in fact, that I think I'll have you do this more often!"

The range of things that people had decided to learn

was amazing, Max said. "I am truly impressed with your determination and your success. Every single one— No, there's someone missing." He turned his head until his gaze rested on Stevie.

"Ms. Lake?"

"Yes?"

"Did you learn something new for today?"

This was not a moment Stevie had been looking forward to. She'd learned something new, all right, but she wasn't eager to share it with the class.

"It's kind of rough," she said.

"Very few things worth learning can be learned quickly," Max said. "Nobody expects expertise. Just show us what you've done so far."

There was no getting out of it. She was going to have to do it, just the way everybody else had. And, after all, it was pretty special, and she had done it all by herself, even if she hadn't done it very well.

"I'll be back," she said. She was hoping it would take her hours to tack up Belle and that everybody would have given up on her by then, but when she returned with the sidesaddle on Belle, they were all waiting, exactly as she had left them.

"Why Stevie, you could have used Diamond!" Tiffani said.

"I wanted to use Belle," Stevie said. "She's my horse."

She led Belle to the mounting block and began what

119

she later considered the most humiliating ten minutes of her life. She and Belle were exactly as good in front of the whole class as they had been by themselves. The only thing that went right was that she didn't fall out of the saddle while she was mounting. After that, there was no good news.

Belle took her usual rightward step when Stevie tried to get her to walk. She finally began moving at a walk and refused to trot. She moved forward, but when Stevie signaled for a left turn, she turned right. She backed up when Stevie tried to stop her, and she trotted when Stevie tried to back her up. Every single attempt at giving Belle an aid backfired, side-fired or front-fired. It was a disaster. Finally, trying to get Belle back to where she could honorably dismount and signal the end of her pitiful demonstration, Stevie kicked her too vigorously. Belle did the only natural thing she could in response. She bucked. Stevie flew out of the saddle, up and over Belle's head, and landed rear-first in the dirt. A perfect end to a perfect demonstration—as long as the title of the demonstration was "Terrible Riding."

Stevie didn't move for a minute, hoping that while she was there on the ground a big hole would open up in the earth and swallow her. That was the only way she could think of that she might not have to face any of her friends or classmates or boyfriend or instructor ever again, which was exactly when she'd be ready to see them.

No hole opened up. Instead she found herself surrounded. Usually Max was the first person to reach a rider who'd been thrown. This time, however, he'd been outpaced by his newest student: Tiffani Thomas.

When Stevie opened her eyes, her gaze was met by Tiffani's pale blue eyes.

"Oh, Stevie!" Tiffani said. "You were wonderful!"

"Huh?"

"Now, don't move," Tiffani said, though Stevie already knew she was to stay still for a while anyway. "Does anything hurt?"

"Nope."

"Can you wiggle your toes?"

Obediently Stevie wiggled her toes and then nodded.

"Stay still and listen to me," Tiffani said. "I know you're fine there, but while you rest a second, I want you to know that you should be really proud of yourself."

"For making an idiot of myself?" Stevie asked.

"No, silly," said Tiffani. "For trying so hard. Everybody else who wanted to learn sidesaddle riding came to me for help. You didn't. You were determined to do it yourself."

"And I really did it, didn't I?" Stevie asked sarcastically.

"You were doing everything right!" Tiffani said.

"Was not!" Stevie protested.

"Well, maybe not exactly right, but you'd figured out what you needed to do and you and Belle were working at it. That sweet ole mare would do just about anything for you, wouldn't she?"

"Like buck me off?" Stevie retorted. She wanted to stand up and get away from this irritating girl. The trouble was that she'd been winded and shaken by the fall. She was all right—nothing was broken, she didn't have a concussion or anything—but she was a prisoner of her own injury for a few minutes and there was no escaping Tiffani.

"You don't understand, do you, Stevie? What you did was brave! Sidesaddle riding is different, and it's a difficult skill for a lot of people. Trying to learn it on your own was a fine thing to do. You learned a lot, too! Oh, sure, what you did here this afternoon wasn't good riding, but you are a good rider and one day you'll be a fine sidesaddle rider. It's a skill, like any other. It takes practice and perhaps some good instruction now and again. I mean, I just happen to be good at it, the same way Max tells me you're good at dressage. I'm a failure at dressage, aside or astride. Tell you what, Stevie, I'll make you a deal. If you'll teach me what you know about dressage, I'll teach you everything I know about sidesaddle."

Stevie blinked and then relaxed back onto the dirt. "You want *me* to teach *you*?"

"Would you?"

Now, *there* was a question. Stevie was suddenly overwhelmed with the realization that all her friends had apparently come to almost the moment they'd met Tiffani Thomas. There was a lot more to this girl than pink jodhpurs. She really knew a lot about horses and really wanted to learn a lot more. She wasn't making it up. Oh, sure, she made statements into questions, but that was mostly a matter of where she came from. She wore funny clothes, but that was who she was, just as Stevie was torn jeans and T-shirts.

"On one condition," Stevie finally answered.

"Name it," said Tiffani.

"That you don't teach me any more about sidesaddle riding."

"Did you hate it?" Tiffani asked.

"Every minute," Stevie told her.

"Some people just do, you know."

"Like me," said Stevie.

She sat up then, and Tiffani gave her a hand to stand up. The class applauded. Carole walked over, leading a bashful Belle, and handed Stevie the reins.

Stevie thanked her and then turned back to Tiffani. "You could do one thing for me," she said.

"Sure."

"Hold the reins while I remount. Max'll kill me if I don't get back in the saddle."

It took only a minute. Stevie mounted, let Tiffani lead Belle in a small circle, and then dismounted. Both she and her horse were ready to return to Belle's stall to remove the hated sidesaddle for a final time.

STEVIE DROPPED THE SIDESADDLE off in the tack room, promising it she would polish it another time. Right then, all she wanted and needed was some time to herself.

It wasn't easy finding a private corner at Pine Hollow. The stable was filled with pumped-up Pony Clubbers. Max's Learn Something New project had been a grand success, and everybody was chattering about what they'd learned or what they wished they'd learned or what someone else—Stevie, mostly—hadn't learned. The barn was no place for quiet contemplation.

Stevie fled to the grain shed.

She found a bale of hay in a corner and sat on it. Thinking always seemed easier on a bale of hay. The first thing she did was to take a quick physical inventory. That fall had been a hard one, and although she was convinced nothing was badly hurt, she knew she was shaken.

Shaken because she'd fallen? No, she fell off Belle fairly regularly. All riders fell off their horses from time to time, and it was no big deal.

It wasn't all that often that she had a chance to fall so spectacularly in front of a large crowd of people. Maybe that was it. She dismissed that, too. It was embarrassing, but everybody else there had done the same thing. Was she embarrassed because she'd been such a miserable failure as a sidesaddle rider? Maybe a little. On the other hand, none of the other sidesaddle riders had excelled. They hadn't been as bad as Stevie, but they were all riding a horse that was experienced. Riding aside was new for both Stevie and Belle. Everybody there knew that. So what was shaking her up?

Stevie ran her fingers through her hair to pull it back from her face. It felt funny. It took her a few seconds to realize that it felt funny because it was all curly. She stood up from the hay bale and walked over to a little mirror that someone had tacked to the wall a long time before.

She barely knew the girl whose reflection greeted her. What was this cloud of curls? Where did the pink sweater come from? Did anyone know who this girl was?

She wasn't anyone Stevie Lake knew, and then Stevie understood that she wasn't anyone that Lisa, Carole, or Phil Marsten knew, either. If Phil liked the real Stevie Lake enough to have been her boyfriend all this time, how could he possibly care about curls and pastels? With a shudder, Stevie sat back down on the bale. She didn't want to see that image in the dusty mirror anymore. And she didn't think anybody who mattered to her did, either.

"I'VE LOOKED EVERYWHERE," Lisa said to Carole. "I don't know where she is."

"Belle's back in her stall, but she hasn't been groomed," Carole said.

"That's a good sign," said Phil, meeting up with Lisa and Carole in the tack room

"How?" asked Carole.

"It means she's still planning on going on the trail ride with us."

"Or that she's so crazed she didn't groom her horse," Lisa suggested.

"Think positive," Carole urged her.

"Okay, then, let's look again. She didn't disappear into thin air!" Phil said.

The three of them went back to the usual starting point for everything at Pine Hollow—the locker room. And there was Stevie, leaning deeply into her locker so that all they could see was her backside, now clad in riding jeans instead of the neatly pressed fawn-colored riding pants she'd had on earlier.

"Stevie?"

"It's me," she said, standing up and turning around. "I knew this was in here somewhere." She had a T-shirt clasped in her hand. "Excuse me a second." She ducked into the bathroom and emerged a few seconds later, wearing the T-shirt and proudly displaying its message: THE HORSE IS THE ONE WITH THE POINTY EARS. "Did someone say 'trail ride'?" she asked brightly.

"Everybody did," said Phil. "Come on, let's get Belle tacked up. You want her usual saddle, don't you?"

"Absolutely!" Stevie said, following Phil into the tack room.

When they were out of earshot, Lisa turned to Carole. "Maybe it was the fall that shook it loose," she said.

"Shook what loose?"

"The alien spirit that took over her body for a while."

Carole slung her arm across Lisa's shoulders. "Maybe," she said. "Maybe not. Our Stevie is sometimes subject to wild swings. This was just one of the wilder ones." She looked at the pink sweater, now abandoned on the bench. That seemed to be a good place for it to stay.

Carole and Lisa met Phil and Stevie at Belle's stall. Tiffani was across the aisle, giving Diamond a final brushing.

"Hey, I'm glad to see you're okay. You disappeared so fast after class, nobody had a chance to help you?"

"I'm fine," Stevie said. "Thanks for coming to my rescue. Say, would you like to come along on our trail ride? We can show you some more of these woods this afternoon."

"Oh, no thanks," Tiffani said. "I've got to get back to my aunt's house. My parents are coming home soon, and I want to get some new clothes to welcome them. My aunt says the mall is great, but I don't know any of the stores there. Have you got any suggestions?"

Without hesitation, and in a single voice, the three girls answered. "Simpson's," they said.

"It must be some store!"

"It is," Stevie assured her.

Carole and Lisa left then to get their horses and told Stevie and Phil they'd meet them at the good-luck horseshoe. Carole also said she'd bring Barq, the horse Phil would be riding, because he was already tacked up.

Stevie slipped the bridle into Belle's mouth and then, smoothing down the reins, found herself on the same side of the big mare as Phil. They were on the far side of the stall door in a rather private corner.

Phil dropped the brush into Belle's grooming bucket and turned to face Stevie. He put his hands on her shoulders, sweeping her hair back from her face.

"You gave us a scare out there," he said.

"It wasn't much of a fall," she said.

"That wasn't what scared us—me, especially. It was all that . . . oh, I don't know. That un-Stevie stuff. You're so special just the way you are that when you start wearing fluff and pink, I don't know what to do."

"I confused you?"

"Yeah," he said.

"I sort of confused myself, too," she said.

"I bet you did."

"But I don't think I'm confused now."

"I hope not."

"What makes you say that?"

"Because I'm about to kiss you, and I wouldn't want to be seen kissing someone who was confused."

"Definitely not confused," Stevie promised.

A few minutes later, as they walked toward their rendezvous with Carole and Lisa, Stevie asked the question that had been bugging her for a while.

"If I'm the girl you like, how come you were flirting with Tiffani?"

"I was?"

"Definitely," Stevie said.

"You're right, I was. But it didn't mean anything."

"Not to you, it didn't."

"But it didn't mean anything to her, either."

"Well, it meant something to me," Stevie told him. "And it hurt."

"I'm sorry," he said. "But it just happened. You see, there are some girls who flirt the way other girls breathe. It's totally natural. And it comes naturally to boys to flirt back, but it doesn't mean anything and it certainly doesn't mean I like her better than I like you, or as well as I like you, or even that I like her at all. It just means that we were flirting, playing a game."

"How do you feel about flirting with me, then?" Stevie asked.

"I love it and it means something," he said.

"That's not logical."

"Neither is the way I feel about you. Want to duck into another stall so that I can remind you?"

"Later, maybe," Stevie said.

Stevie hadn't felt this good for weeks. Not since the day Tiffani arrived. Even though the sky was overcast, she would have sworn the weather was perfect. Even though Belle was still moody after her unsatisfactory stint as a sidesaddle horse, Stevie would have sworn she was the nicest, most obedient horse in Virginia. And even though the trail ride lasted more than an hour, Stevie would have sworn it flew by in less than fifteen minutes.

The friends rode all around the hillside and then came down to their favorite spot by the edge of the creek. By the time they settled onto the rock, where they resisted the temptation to dangle their toes in the too-cold water, their conversation turned to shopping.

"Poor Tiffani," Lisa said. "She's not going to find a thing left for her at Simpson's!"

"Aw, c'mon," Stevie protested. "My mother didn't let me buy everything. Remember the mint outfit?"

"I don't think mint will go with her pale blue eyes," Carole said.

Stevie gave her a withering look.

"Well, if she has trouble finding things there, I might have a few items in my wardrobe I could share with her."

"You mean like your LIFE IS UNCERTAIN. EAT DESSERT FIRST T-shirt with the rip in the sleeve?"

"How about the green one with the big red paint smear on it?" Lisa suggested.

"It's not a big smear," said Stevie. "You can barely see it."

"Not unless you happen to be looking at the shirt from within, say, fifty yards," Carole said.

"Okay, what would you give her?" Phil asked.

"I have this white angora sweater," Stevie said. "But it's really worn out. . . ."

"Holes?

"Nope."

"Rips?"

"Not exactly."

132

"What do you mean, 'worn out'?" Phil asked.

"Well, it's not worn *out* so much as just plain *worn*. What I mean is that it's gotten all the wearing it's going to get from me!"

Lisa, Carole, and Phil all reached to give Stevie hugs at the same time. It was nice to have her back.

ABOUT THE AUTHOR

BONNIE BRYANT is the author of more than a hundred books about horses, including The Saddle Club series, Saddle Club Super Editions, and the Pony Tails series. She has also written novels and movie novelizations under her married name, B. B. Hiller.

Ms. Bryant began writing The Saddle Club in 1986. Although she had done some riding before that, she intensified her studies then and found herself learning right along with her characters Stevie, Carole, and Lisa. She claims that they are all much better riders than she is.

Ms. Bryant was born and raised in New York City. She still lives there, in Greenwich Village, with her two sons.